The Extra Large Medium

The Extra Large Medium
Helen Slavin

POCKET
BOOKS

LONDON • SYDNEY • NEW YORK • TORONTO

First published in the USA by Black Cat, 2007
An imprint of Grove/Atlantic, Inc.
First published in Great Britain by Pocket Books UK, 2007
An imprint of Simon & Schuster UK Ltd
A CBS COMPANY

1 3 5 7 9 10 8 6 4 2

Simon & Schuster UK Ltd
Africa House
64–78 Kingsway
London WC2B 6AH

Simon & Schuster Australia
Sydney

www.simonsays.co.uk

A CIP catalogue record for this book is available
from the British Library

ISBN-13: 978-1-84739-122-3

Printed and bound in Great Britain by
Cox & Wyman Ltd, Reading, Berks

For Dad, who started the race,
and Stephen, who took up the baton.

I don't get to see Heaven. Once, there was an unseemly tussle with what I think was an angel. Muscular. Lots of feathers. It was pushing against the other side of a door. That's what I chiefly see. Doors. Not the huge gothic style doors hewn from oak that you might imagine. Not Pearly Gates either. Bog standard blank doors. Made from MDF.

Angels are intimidating. The bouncers of Heaven. At least that is the message I get from a lot of my clients. The angels aren't keen on dead people communicating with living people. Once you're dead the angels think you cross a line and that in fact a line should be drawn under you. Or possibly a cross over you.

You should put up and shut up. You've had your time. You've said your piece.

Which brings me to me. I have always been able to hear the Dead speak. That makes it sound very high-flown, as if I am some semi-celestial messenger tap-dancing up and down that staircase they had in *A Matter of Life and Death* with a series of life or death communications.

What I should say is that I have always been able to listen to dead people whingeing on, moaning and groaning (without chains) about the myriad petty gripes and grumbles of life. That is the key. If your Aunt Mildred was a sour old bat when she was alive the addition of harp lessons and a cloud is not going to turn her into a philosopher.

It has been my experience that most dead people who come back to haunt others, or in fact pester me, do so because they've got some unfinished business of a particularly tedious sort. Lost cats, squabbles over wills, Crown Derby coffee sets and leather pouffes are about the limits of it. No one has anything earth shattering to say. I exist as a kind of customer service department, running a stream of endless errands just to keep these people quiet.

I'm on the side of the angels. Shut up is what I say. Or else tell me what it's like. Tell me something. Anything. Protect me.

Chocolate brown childhood

A s a kid I used to see a lot of people who wore chocolate brown clothing. As a kid, I accepted this as the norm. I thought that chocolate brown was a very popular colour for clothing.

Chocolate brown is the new black. They don't wear black in Heaven apparently. I don't know what they wear because, as stated, I get the door in my face. But when you aren't quite checked into your parking space behind the pearly gates you get to moon about in chocolate brown.

In Hell they all wear evening gowns. Heavily boned bodices. Dress-shirt collars just that bit too tight. Your forehead just that bit too sweaty and the perspiration running like an itching, infuriating river down from your armpit into the elastic of your knickers. The point where it pinches your waistband.

So…I imagined that the brown-clothed people could be seen and heard by everyone. When I was five My Mother thought that I had an imaginary friend called, unlikely I know, Mrs Berry. My Mother accepted her existence completely. This was one of those phases that children go through.

Mrs Berry sat and knitted chocolate brown scarves and mittens and hideous bobbled hats at our kitchen table. She talked to me about household tips and gossip about friends and neighbours who were themselves long dead. She grumbled about being dead not because she missed being alive, or kisses, or the smell of the earth after a summer rainstorm. No, Mrs Berry thought being dead was very inconvenient because she couldn't bottom the house.

'Bottom the house'. It was her favourite phrase. Her joy was to clean and scour from attic to cellar (if we'd had one). Not for her the fragrances of Chanel or even a bottle of Tweed. No. Mrs Berry liked Ajax and Dolly Blue.

I suppose it is a measure of My Mother that she did not find it in the least odd that when I talked about Mrs Berry I talked about the war and household chores and the suet pudding recipe in this week's *Woman's Weekly*. It never occurred to her to think 'Where is Annie getting all this?' But then we had Patrice staying with us and she pretty much only had eyes for him. He was a student from Toulouse. I don't remember very much about him except that he taught me to say 'Bonjour'.

The things he taught My Mother were many and myriad. As a child I had not realised that there are two worlds that we live in, the world that everyone sees on the outside, Living Room World, and the world that only you see on the inside. The world of closed bedroom doors and wet weekends in Tunbridge Wells. At seven I was being tutored in the fine arts of Brasso and starch by a woman who had been dead for forty years and My Mother, who was supposed to be schooling me in the ways of bedtime stories and the safe castle that should be your home, was being tutored in fellatio by a man probably half her age.

In fact if I really think about it, and trust me I don't, she was probably tutoring him. He was after all a student, not more than eighteen. Who knows what My Mother's sexual history was before my birth? It was chequered as a chess board after me. It would have been psychedelic if I hadn't happened along to cramp her style.

You're not really allowed to say that are you? Not in the Living Room World. You're supposed to think that your mother, and indeed, if you have one, your father, are next to the angels. They don't get it wrong. Then you grow up yourself and realise that parents are irrevocably human too. I look back now and wonder at how I ever trusted My Mother with anything. She was, after all, as loopy and dangerous as I am now. If I ever manage to have any children I shall tell them at the outset, 'Don't trust me, I'm lost and afraid too. I have NO IDEA.'

What Patrice did teach her was how to cook. The growth of garlic in our back garden and a herb trough are testament to that. I still cannot smell lemon thyme and not think of him and his soft voice, his strange words. I imagine that My Mother smelt lemon thyme and thought of his kisses, or the touch of his hand, hot and sweaty on the cool marble of her backside.

For me, however, there was also a third world, no pun intended. This third world was the Waiting Room of Heaven World.

Things arrived at breaking point when Mrs Berry could no longer keep her rather unkind remarks about My Mother's housekeeping abilities to herself.

My Mother had a lot of abilities and quite frankly I have never blamed her for not nurturing that one. My Mother cleaned the bath out with dirty laundry. She did not red raddle steps, clean windows with vinegar and scrim cloths or turn her mattresses. Instead she had a good time, giving her mattresses adequate exercise with sweaty sexual excesses.

I argued with Mrs Berry. She got angry and broke a teapot. Shoved it clean off the worktop. It smashed at my feet.

My Mother, who was eating pickled beetroot out of the jar at the time, saw the whole thing, saw the teapot lift in the air and smash down without any help from me. I cried, 'I didn't do it…it was Mrs Berry…' And we went to sleep at Aunt Mag's for the night. Even Patrice. I don't think there was a three-in-a-bed-and-the-little-one-said situation. Not knowing my Aunt Mag as I did.

But there, I have foxed my own argument. I did not know my Aunt Mag. I knew the Living Room World of Aunt Mag. The ciggie smoking, grumbling old baggage in too-tight jumpers with too-done, candy floss hair.

It was an odd night at Aunt Mag's. I often spent Thursday nights there. More on that later. But those Thursdays were taken up with Aunt Mag smoking and me eating her supply of garibaldi biscuits and blowing the skin off the instant hot chocolate that she always made for me.

I have to confess that I didn't much care for instant hot chocolate. It was always chalky and sweet but it was something I did that was different. It was peculiar to Aunt Mag's and so, even though it was disgusting and coated my teeth with a chocolate brown fuzzy feeling, I enjoyed it. It was part of my tapestry.

On the night we stayed there with Patrice there was no hot chocolate. Aunt Mag poured My Mother a stiff whisky and they sat in front of the telly with the sound turned down. Their faces were illuminated by the flickering white light as they knocked back the amber coloured liquid from little shot glasses. They looked like women who should have been in a saloon with John

Wayne. Only of course he would have put them across his knee for such wanton behaviour.

I stood at the bottom of the stairs watching them through the glass pane in the living-room door. I couldn't hear what they were saying, only vague mumbles which seemed all to be scared or anxious—there were no comforting mumbles that night. My Aunt Mag shuddered and shook ash all over her clothes. She swiped at it with her hand. As she did so she caught sight of me out of the corner of her eye and screamed. My Mother looked up and screamed too before they realised it was me.

My life had become a ghost story. I was a Midwich Cuckoo.

Mum's Eye View:
sideways on

Is this on? What do I do? Just talk?...

She was scary as a kid, Annie. She was scary before she was born. I was young and wild and untamed. Untrained really for anything. No one told me about men. You know, they don't come with a handbook or an instruction manual. I got what they'd call 'hands on' training then. Their hands. On.

When she...when I was...You didn't really say the word 'pregnant' either. It was like 'Nazi' or 'bum', you just didn't use the word.

It's always been hard for a single mum except in the war when they were the home front, and even then I get the impression they were expected to be saintly. Not go dancing. How dare you go dancing when your husband is off fighting?

Go dancing is what I'd've said. He's fighting for your right to dance. Dance because he is fighting.

I think the Virgin Mary has a lot to answer for myself. But then, what do we really know about her, eh? Only what's siphoned through the Bible. My God and I think I had a scary kid...

You're not born a mum. It's a trade you have to learn you know, like being a blacksmith. Only I think that a blacksmith eventually works out how to make the horseshoes or the wrought-iron fencing whereas, being a mother, a parent I should say, you're never finished. You're always the apprentice and let's face it, the kid is always your master.

I don't believe much in nurture. I believe in love. But I believe you are what you are, ready made, in a parcel. The wrapping just gets torn off as you go. Some people are a diamond tiara. Others are Christmas socks.

With my girl...she came out a bit like a woolly jumper knitted by your Aunt Alice. You aren't sure at first but then you put it on and it truly was made for you. It keeps you warm. It smells like home.

There's terror and fear and hatred and resentment and all the things they never tell you. But that day when I found out about… when I knew, I thought I'd let her down. I didn't know how to protect her, how to fix this for her. I felt useless. I thought she'd grow out of it. I hoped.

Because someone was in our house talking to my daughter. Picking on my daughter. Someone I couldn't see. An intruder. You can't sleep for thinking, well what is she saying and doing now? So you go to the single mother of them all and you ask her for advice.

And after all that talk of Faith—they don't Believe, you know.

Bell, book, candle

MRS BERRY. That was the giveaway. Her name, Mrs Berry. My Mother found out that Mrs Berry had lived in our house some forty years previously. My Mother confessed to my Aunt Mag that a whole series of petty but unexplained events, moving soap, folded tea towels, a rug moving across the room, could all now be put down to Mrs Berry bearing a forty-year housekeeping grudge towards the subsequent mortgagees of her home. For forty years Mrs Berry had denied herself the pleasures of Heaven because no one was putting enough Domestos in the toilet. Small minded doesn't cover it.

My Mother decided to have the house exorcised and the priest, Father Tansy, was called in.

Father Tansy arrived with his bell, book and candle and he droned his way through some prayers sprinkling holy water everywhere, which just about drove Mrs Berry batty. I watched as she followed him around with a chocolate brown dishcloth trying to contain the mess. 'Priests,' she grumbled before moving the soap from the left side of the kitchen sink to the right. My Mother and Father Tansy were up in the attic by then, casting demons out of the bric à brac and undiscovered antiquities that were stashed there.

Lesson Number One. Other people's junk often comes with other people. It is unfinished business of the first water. Stuff they have left undone and will spend centuries trying to do. Some people cannot leave it alone. It's like leaving the grill on, they get halfway up that stairway to Heaven and they remember, 'Oh my God, I've left that Picasso in the attic...our Gerard will never find it under the insulation...I'll just be a minute.' But a minute is an eternity and no one ever finds the Picasso under the insulation because no one can hear them.

Except me. I know what is down the back of your sofa. I have been told about the shed keys dropped under the floorboards in the dining room. I have been told about those keys some thirty-five years after that shed has been destroyed to make way for a pre-fab garage.

My Mother had a lot of sleepless nights after my encounter with Mrs Berry. Already I was being shown the way. I had to keep further encounters from My Mother. I should not worry her like this. I did not want to make her afraid.

At seven I was in Miss Hadley's class at school. It was an old school, built in Victorian times with high windows like a prison. On one corridor there was a stock room with a heavy dark blue door that had a grille set into the bottom of it. This room was stacked high with pots of glue and sugar paper, exercise books, pencil erasers, pencils and poster paints. It had its own strange aroma and I did not like it. I did not like to walk past it.

One afternoon I was sent to fetch some sugar paper and some

gummed squares and I found out why I didn't like the cupboard.

There was a brown-clad boy in there. Albert. He had been locked in there in 1896 and had suffocated. His teacher, Miss Whitemarsh, had shut him up in there as a punishment for not having boots and she had forgotten about him. It had been raining and she had been offered a lift home by a handsome butcher who was courting her. It was only later over a dinner of pork chops that she remembered Albert. By then it was too late.

The courts did not look kindly on Miss Whitemarsh for suffocating her pupil. Miss Whitemarsh was hanged by the neck until dead and the Education Authority had a ventilation grille fitted into the heavy blue door. Which explained the brown-clad lady I had seen walking up and down the corridor every day since I arrived at the school.

At the age of seven I reminded Miss Whitemarsh where she had left Albert. In letting him out she let them both go. It was the first time I had seen a real ghost, as the two faded from chocolate brown to an ethereal grey before disappearing into a shaft of sunlight and dust motes cast from the high windows.

My Mother didn't encourage me at all. My Mother, through her own fears, did not want me chit-chatting with the Dead. It was forbidden. After she had Mrs Berry exorcised, she put it out of her mind as a phase I would grow out of. Her fear made me afraid, although no one ever tried to hurt me. Bore me, possibly.

And I felt that this strange Waiting Room of Heaven World was something I did wrong. It was a bad naughtiness but I couldn't rid myself of it. It didn't matter if I didn't listen to these people, they kept pushing at me. They woke me in the night shouting into my ear so that I would sit bolt upright amongst the blankets, sweating into the darkness, only to be told some tedious nonsense from Mrs Ordsall about pruning some fruit tree. Or there was the very persistent Mr Knightley. 'Have they bought that grand piano yet? Did you tell them what I said about Winchley's and that upright? Did you tell them?'

I have often wondered whether Mr Knightley's relatives ever bought that grand piano or if they took his proper advice and plumped for the upright.

It was Aunt Mag who thought I should be encouraged. She said that being a medium ran in the family. That my Great-uncle Sidney had once rolled out of the snug at the Claybank and into a spiritualist meeting. Him and a group of belching, farting mates spilling out of the pub into the rain, all eager for somewhere to keep warm whilst waiting for the bus.

The lights from the Spiritualist Church across the road were golden. It was the most golden light that Uncle Sidney had ever seen. And before you get too bowled over and start interpreting Destiny, Fate and the Intervention of Angels, you should remember that my Great-uncle Sidney was, as he put it, 'Three sheets and a couple of patchwork quilts to the wind.'

'We could hole up in there for half an hour,' he said, and made to twist the brass doorhandle. A golden, glittering orb. Down to the polishing endeavours of Mrs Berry as it happened.

'Not going in there,' Hugh shivered into his elder brother's best jacket, brought out for funerals and pub crawling. 'Full of old bags. Bunch of table tappers. My mam says to keep away.'

The others turned at this.

'Your mam?' Gerald sniggered, blowing a ribbon of snot from his nose.

'It's dabbling in the occult. Steer clear. They'll have you stripped naked and sacrificed to virgins...'

Recommendation enough to Sidney and Gerald.

Inside the church was cold and damp. A huge patch of mildew marked the wall between the two tall leaded windows at the front end. It looked like a map of some distant country. The country of the Dead. A continent strewn with black mildew forests and long, silver rivulets of effervescence. On the dais, against a backdrop of folded chairs and a collapsible ping-pong table, a man in a dark blue suit appeared to be asleep in a hard-backed chair. The rest of the hard chairs had been set out in the hall. A handful of people were parked across them. At least that's what everyone else saw.

My Great-uncle Sidney had not been up for a spiritual encounter. If anything, he was up for a laugh at the expense of these sad gits waiting to find out about Crown Derby coffee sets and shed keys. But one of the first things he noticed about the church was how many people were wearing chocolate brown clothing. It struck him so much he mentioned it to a blowsy-looking woman sitting nearby. She didn't mind his beer breath and smiled when he asked if chocolate brown was the uniform.

'Jim,' the man onstage, that evening's medium, seemed to jolt awake, 'I've a Jim here, or possibly he's looking for a Jim?' He looked to his audience for answers. There was a nervous tensing of shoulders but no definite response. The medium onstage pushed on, determined. 'Might be a Tim. I've got a crackly line tonight…it must be the weather…Tim or a Jim?'

The man in the chocolate brown suit beside Sidney tapped him on the shoulder then.

'Why don't you help the bugger out?' he said gesturing wearily at the medium. Sidney was mellow with pale ale. Happy to oblige.

'How can I help?'

Another brown-clad man with a frustrated expression stood up at the front and looked back at Sidney. 'Well for a start it isn't

Jim. It's Viv. I want to speak to Viv and I've been waiting hours and not getting anywhere. He isn't bloody listening.' The brown-clad man at the front was getting very irate.

'Who's Viv then? This one?' Sidney moved down a couple of rows and pointed at the woman, touched her shoulder. She stiffened as if her blood had suddenly turned to quick-setting concrete. Everyone else was holding their breath, although Sidney did not notice. The brown-clad man at the front nodded.

'At last. Tell her I knew all along…'

'Why don't you tell her?' Sidney asked, not wanting to interfere in a marital tiff.

'You do it…you tell her. I knew, and if she wants him she's to have him and never mind what your mother says, Viv. Get away from your ma, Viv. Get away. Let him take you.'

Hugh and Gerald sobered up sharpish as they watched my Great-uncle Sidney talk to the air. Everyone got their message that night. Everyone.

The blowsy woman beside him did not mind when Uncle Sidney reeled sideways and vomited into her lap. The blowsy woman was Kitty. She was never officially my Great-aunt Kitty because my Great-uncle Sidney never officially married her. He was still officially married to my Great-aunt Edna. But you don't get a ceremony and a certificate for being the true love of someone's life.

Kitty convinced him when he sobered up.

Sidney woke up next morning to the fizzing of Andrews Liver Salts and the sight of Kitty in a Japanese kimono that had actually come from Japan. It was celadon green with a golden dragon embroidered onto the back. His tail trailed down one sleeve and he breathed silver wire and gold-leaf fire down the other. Sidney drank the liver salts and ate bacon and eggs as Kitty laughed at him.

Sidney had no idea what fairy story he might have to concoct to cover this absence from home. He was not in love with his wife but he had never stayed away or been with another woman. Sidney was a man of promises. You keep them.

'You haven't a clue, have you, what we did last night?'

Sidney shook his head, put his knife and fork neatly together on the empty plate.

'Good,' she said leaning into him, 'I'll always be able to hold it against you.' Her bosom seemed to inflate before him like a lifejacket. He never wanted to let go.

'Call in sick,' Kitty told him.

She took him to the museum after he called in sick to work. He was against calling in sick. He was an honest, hard-working bloke of a man. Kitty simply laughed. Sidney didn't think it would be very funny when he got the sack but Kitty just laughed again. 'I'm going to show you the way,' she said, and for the bus journey into town Great-uncle Sidney thought he'd been kidnapped by a Jesus freak.

She took him into the upper gallery of the museum building so he could look down on the main concourse. It was a grand Gothic building, a gift to the city from local boy made million-aire Sir Charles Whitworth. It was called the Alice Museum after his wife.

Kitty simply stood there with Sidney and asked him who he could see. Sidney looked down on a party of schoolkids drawing on worksheets as they sat and sprawled on the Victorian tiled flooring. Then he saw the brown-clad Sir Charles bustling about in and out of the offices and up and down the stairwells.

Sir Charles never fulfilled his plans. The museum was never finished to the drawings. He was doomed now to spend his eternity trying to finish it his way. There was a brown-clad workman who had died whilst fitting the roof bosses in the vaulted ceiling. He was up a ladder still. Sir Charles chided him from the bottom of it, left a bit, right a bit…you're going to chip it doing that.

Not that Sidney believed this until Kitty sat him down in the library with some documentary evidence. Photographs of Sir Charles, his obituary in the local paper.

Sidney got the sack from the inkworks. But he made his million as Sidney Colville, the Extra Large Medium.

STOP.

Hail fellow well met on the highway to madness. Madness is a small town not very far away. Most of us, at some point, find we could probably walk there. Others have the road cave in and dump them there.

Sidney was a grown-up when he first tuned in. He had to make the effort and alcohol let him do that. He could tune out. He had to ask them. Me, I had an open frequency right from the start.

No one believes in magic anymore. If you hear voices in your head then it is simply cost effective to address the imbalances in your brain with a concoction from the chemical companies. I learnt that voices are not in your head if what they say leads you into real life. If what they tell you is a true story. If what they tell you is the ending to their true story. If they send you messages that match up, you are not mad. You are a messenger.

I didn't tell My Mother about the chocolate brown brigade after Mrs Berry. I, like all children, did not want to worry her. I loved her, I did not want her to be afraid. I did not want her to be afraid of me. I could dream in nightmares but I wouldn't tell. I learnt quickly to adjust responses so that I wasn't ever caught out talking to someone who effectively wasn't there.

School became a safer haven after I helped Miss Whitemarsh.

She and Albert disappeared, said their goodbye. The everyday streets were more of a problem. We lived in a town that had been begun by the Romans. A walk to McNab's to buy shoes was a living history experiment. I longed to live in a purpose-built town where I imagined there would be no history. No unfinished business.

History. Be interested. It is where we come from, it is where we are, it is where we are going. I learnt Latin from a Roman soldier.

Aunt Mag and her encouragement nearly finished me before I had begun.

Thursdays

ON THURSDAYS I always stayed with Aunt Mag. She was My Mother's eldest sister and lived closest. There were two other sisters. One, Lorna, had a farm in the Lake District (no, I never got to talk to Wordsworth or Beatrix Potter). Another, Marjorie, lived in America. We all imagined she lived a Hollywood style of life with chocolate malteds, ballgames and Buicks. It transpired she lived like Davy Crockett only not quite so civilised.

So I stayed with Aunt Mag. I enjoyed this at first. She let me off the leash more than My Mother. She had a bigger house. A piano-shaped jewel box filled with glittering finds that flashed and burned.

Thursday was the day Mr Bentley came to visit, you see. I did not know Mr Bentley although he knew more than he wanted to about me. At an early stage in my life there was a rumour that he might have been My Father. A rumour he scotched by showing people his vasectomy scars.

Mr Bentley sold soap around the country. He travelled in a company car and on Thursdays he visited My Mother. They did not discuss soap. Mr Bentley was one of her earlier sexual excesses. He put the first ten thousand miles on My Mother's new mattress. He gave her bars of soap as love tokens. She had a cupboard under the stairs which was stocked with seemingly never-ending bars of soap. Even twenty years after Mr Bentley's departure we were still using up his soaps. Lily of the valley, lavender, bergamot...

Mr Bentley's penis. The starting pistol.

Aunt Mag didn't buy a ouija board. She made one. It made it more sinister eventually. If it had been bought from a shop with 'Made in China' typed on the underside, it would have seemed fake and destructible. A board game. A joke. But it was indestructible. Wherever I hid it, however I damaged it or burnt it or screwed it up, Aunt Mag could always get out her pen and draw another.

They got cross. I was too slow. I was a child after all. I didn't understand some of the things I was told. They were not people we knew, which Aunt Mag found very hard to take. She had an idea that my open frequency 'gift' was restricted to family members only, and when her own mother didn't care to speak with her but some strange ex-librarian popped up to say hello she got shirty. Then it occurred to her that there might be a bit of pin money to be made from these communications with other people's relatives.

Not to be disrespectful to my Aunt Mag but the woman had a serious smoking habit that sometimes ran to Havana cigars and one eye, at all times, on the horses. Horses were the love of my Aunt Mag's life. She never loved anything as much as racehorses. She loved their names, her two all-time favourites being Red Rum and a lesser-known nag by the name of Cherish the Day. Red Rum did his share of winning. Cherish the Day did just cherish all his days, and spent the greater part of his existence eating and standing about, occasionally plucking up the energy to sit a silk-clad jockey on his back and put a shift on at Little Roodee.

Cherish the Day was a handsome horse and my Aunt Mag loved him. I don't know, because I never asked her, but looking back I don't doubt for a moment that she was 'in love' with Cherish the Day. She took taxi rides out to the stables to see him train and at one point was having an affair with his owner. Val Hartman was a big, meaty bloke. Would probably have styled himself as a stallion. I have often wondered if, when she was between the sheets with Val Hartman, she was imagining rolling in the hay with Cherish the Day.

She got a hare-brained scheme. It was one of those schemes like the things we think up as kids. You will save up really hard and travel to London to see the Queen. Or perhaps you'll save up really hard and buy an aeroplane and a parachute and you'll watch a lot of films about flying and pick up tricks and read some handbooks about being a pilot so that you'll have a good basic knowledge and before the grown-ups know anything about it you'll be skimming over the rooftops in a Cessna. Only of course, being a kid you get utterly distracted and the following month you're saving up to buy a lifetime's supply of Hubba-Bubba bubble gum.

Aunt Mag's scheme was like that. She would hold séances at her house every Thursday and she would make enough money to buy herself a racehorse. Then, with the continuation of the séances she would be earning enough, tax free, to keep the racehorse in the manner to which it would become accustomed.

Racehorses like a luxury lifestyle. Woolly blankets, rolled oats, only the finest home-grown carrots and Cox's orange pippins.

She had a large network of friends which spread through the bingo club and the local pubs where she was a regular, the Freemasons, the Claybank, the Robin Hood and the Hark to Towler to name but a few. Then there was a second wave of pals who she knew through her job at the textile factory. She was the floor supervisor in the machining department. They sewed odd-shaped bits of things. A consignment of sleeves here, a shipment of left legs there. The brims of rain hats, the quilting for sleeping bags.

I think Aunt Mag was a hard taskmistress because no one we met from her workplace ever seemed pleased to see her. Then again it could simply have been that the factory affected the people that worked there in that way. It could also have been that they came to work at that factory because they were like that. Cause and effect. Symptom and cure.

Aunt Mag had her little side office on the factory floor which reeked of cigarettes and mints. If she wasn't sucking on a cigarette she was sucking on a mint. She ate the huge extra strong ones that were like pieces of chalk and burned your mouth. She was brisk and efficient at best; mean and bullying at worst.

The very first Thursday she charged everyone fifty pence. Seven of her workmates rolled up at the house and were a bit taken aback at the sight of me. They hadn't expected a kid, it seemed.

'I hadn't expected a kid,' said a dark-haired woman with tightly coiled hair. It was oiled in some way, slicked and shiny in a car-grease sort of way. She looked as if she'd had a bath and combed her hair and washed her face and then just absent mindedly headed out. As if she had forgotten some vital part of herself, her face. She was washed out and greasy. Her name I remember was Bar. Short for Barbara.

There was also Kaz (short for Karen), Al (Alison) and Dot. They all had shortened names as if they couldn't be bothered being the whole person. Then there was Gail. Gail with eyes like a sheep. Hair like a sheep too, in rough-looking tight curls around her head. She played with her earrings a lot, twirling and twirling at the gold loop as if it was an aerial and she couldn't quite get the picture.

It was very successful. We didn't need to draw the curtains and pitch ourselves into darkness that day. We just sat down after some tea and biscuits and Mr Kipling cakes and straight away there was a queue of people. Trace and Al started off giggling and joking around and lost interest very quickly. I think this was chiefly because they couldn't spell. Bar seemed very anxious. Her already strained face seemed to get tighter, as if her skull was trying to push out through the skin and get on with the job. But no one wanted to talk to Bar.

There was someone looking for Jim. There is always someone looking for Jim. More on that later.

Then Dot's brother declared his love for her and suddenly everyone was interested. Trace and Al shut up sharpish. Bar slackened up a bit and looked into the middle distance. I was too young to notice it then, but Bar could not look at Dot. She wanted to absent herself, to save Dot the embarrassment. And there was a fair bit of embarrassing information. It was like some other-worldly soap opera. Dot sat and sobbed quietly as her brother spoke of how he missed her, the touch of her skin, the kiss of her lips…and how he had loved her so very much.

Dot had always lived with her brother, it seemed. No one had thought much about it; if anything they had considered that Dot and Dan were a couple of sad sacks who couldn't break out of the family home. All the time people pitied them buying their small tins of beans and their white tin loaf in the bakers, and it turned out that one of the greatest passions of all time was happening in their house.

Now her workmates were being told intimate details of their relationship. Daniel didn't hold back that evening. He said what he felt and he said it straight from his no-longer-beating heart. Dot didn't seem to care at the time, what she cared about was being able to tell her brother, Daniel, what she was feeling and how she missed him and to make him a promise, that she'd never find anyone else.

'Promise you'll remember me, Dorothy?…You'll never go looking for someone else…'

Even at my tender age I thought this was a bit harsh and he was very insistent. 'I'll be waiting for you. You know that. However long it takes I'll be here,' he promised.

He extracted that promise from a weeping Dorothy. She didn't hear what anyone else said, it was as if it was just her and Daniel in my Aunt Mag's back room. They all sat and took in the information.

Later Gail would use it against Dot. Dot had applied for a job at the library and an unknown informant wrote a letter saying that Dot was a reprobate who had spent a lifetime shagging her brother. It was the use of the word 'shagging' that gave the game away really. Everyone knew it was Gail. It wasn't even revenge for there was nothing that Dot had done to get on Gail's bad side. It was pleasure. It was evil.

I don't think you can say that Gail's life made her evil, her hard times made her do things that were less than nice. I think that she was just like that. She was hard like a stone. A woman with granite for a skeleton. If she had been the Duchess of Argyll or suddenly been made Queen of the Netherlands she would still have had that mean streak.

Our Thursday sessions strengthened and Aunt Mag took to drawing the curtains and lighting candles for atmosphere. I didn't really need the ouija board and it slowed things down but she kept it for effect. She began charging a whole pound but several people got their money back when they didn't get a personal message.

They looked at me strangely, those women, as if I was a freak, a thing to be afraid of.

Except for Bar. After that first week Bar came along every week and she had a different look about her. She was waiting for something and it wasn't coming. She had a way of raising one eyebrow. Her eyebrows were shaved and painted in pencil. The effect was to make her face look even more forgotten, as if someone had been painting it and got as far as her eyebrows before finding that they'd let a pan boil dry and being distracted.

When we had finished the session Bar was always the last to go. As Aunt Mag was seeing everyone out Bar would sit and finish a smoke. She didn't say anything to me, she just waited. But there was nothing. No one in chocolate brown slacks and chocolate brown sweater had anything to say to her. Then she would pull on her jacket, a crumpled leather coat that made her look even thinner. She would stub out her cigarette in the ashtray and leave.

And then one week the message came. A slight lady in a chocolate brown shirtwaist dress pushed her way forwards before Bar had even got her coat off. Trace and Al weren't there yet and Aunt Mag was in the kitchen with three other women from her bingo club. They were hopeless, they came along expecting racing tips and Nostradamus-style predictions. They wanted to know who was going to win the World Cup or the Grand

National. They didn't get it. They didn't see that the point was the chocolate brown lady in the shirtwaist dress.

She was so anxious to get the message over with that she didn't wait. She stepped in and spoke. Bar had her back to me at the time and to suddenly hear her mother's voice was a big shock.

'Barbara. Listen. I can't stay long.'

Barbara turned to face me. Today she had forgotten to pencil in her eyebrows.

'Stick with Kath.'

Bar stared at me. All my body was prickling now and I was willing Bar to say what she wanted before her mother headed off through the MDF door to Heaven.

'Kath.'

'You've found someone, Bar. That's the point. Stick with her.'

And then I was on the floor and full of pins and needles. Bar didn't take her coat off. She picked up her bag from the chair and headed out, pushing past Aunt Mag to get there.

It is no credit to my Aunt Mag that instead of seeing that I was in a bit of a state she simply picked me up off the floor, fed me a glass of brandy and let me carry on. There were three messages about Crown Derby tea sets that afternoon and they weren't connected with anyone there. Someone was still looking for Jim and the three women from the bingo club never did get to find out who was going to win the National.

A horse died in the National that year. It was put down at the trackside and Aunt Mag sobbed even though it wasn't Cherish the Day. Aunt Mag was not interested in the fate of the jockey, who at one point was thought to have broken his neck. The horse was. Two days later that horse, which was chocolate brown to start off with, came to see me. And that horse was worried about the jockey.

Bar is still with Kath all these years later. I see them in town and Bar always gives me a nod. That nod is worth more than a thousand Crown Derby tea sets.

After a while I began to dread Thursdays. It was hard work. I felt very tired on Friday morning and I had bad dreams on Thursday nights, as well as bad dreams on Wednesday nights in anticipation of the events of Thursday. I refused to go to Aunt Mag's on several occasions. My Mother resented this. I was cramping her style. Impinging on her last freedom. Her fling.

Finally someone was so furious he didn't go away. We were having our usual session. The ladies from the bingo club were there that week and a new girl from the factory, Abby. She was very quiet and didn't like it when we shut the curtains and lit the candles. I had to admit I'd never liked that either. It made it sinister. Aunt Mag made a big thing of drawing up the ouija board, as if she was casting a spell, invoking the Devil.

It certainly felt like that when Hal arrived. He was very tall, very angry and the words he used to me were all ones that I was forbidden. I couldn't tell Aunt Mag what was being said because it was unrepeatable. I held tight to the upturned cup we used as a pointer. I wouldn't budge it. In the end I said I felt sick. She was furious. Her mates asked for their money back. Jim was, once again, not found.

I got home still feeling very odd with Hal poking at my shoulder, bickering at me. My Mother had had her evening with Mr Bentley and was stacking up a couple of boxes of Imperial Leather. I went to bed. Hal kept me awake all night with his anxiety and his distress.

'I thought you fucking listened. Why aren't you listening to me?' and he began to shake me. I lay very still and quiet under the blankets, hoping that if I stayed rigid and quiet he would be fooled into thinking I wasn't there. Hoped. Hoped. Imagined.

What if I stopped breathing? If I could hold on for long enough, could I work the ultimate magic and disappear? And just when I couldn't hold on any longer, when I thought it was quiet and perhaps he was gone, he would tug at my feet. The ultimate bogeyman, hanging onto my ankles. Have you ever been so scared you couldn't scream?

I worked very hard at ignoring him. He followed me around, swearing at me, grabbing at me. The first one ever to do that. To ever actually reach out and make contact. Pins and needles in my arm when he touched me.

I was eleven. I have tried to forget this for a long time. A quarter century, in fact. You can't blame him really. Like Hugh's mam warned, we were dabbling in the occult. I was too young and untrained to deal with these people and their emotional turmoils. For Hal it was like getting to the front of the queue at last only to be told he was in the wrong shop.

Hal's unfinished business was that he had been murdered. I have never found out who it was who killed him or whether they were ever punished. Something happened eventually because he stopped visiting me. He no longer had unfinished business. If the law didn't catch up with his killer in this life then certainly those too-tight dress shirts and the pinch-feet lace-up dress shoes would have done.

I was in school. It was the summer term of my first year at the secondary school, Sir Charles Whitworth High School. Sounds fancy on purpose so that prospective parents would be lulled into a false sense of security. Its real name should have been Strangeways. Like the prison. It was a petri dish of a school. You had to fight your way through the kids who were fungus or poison.

My first year was not going well. I was quite bright, quite

quiet, I got on with what I was asked to do. I didn't make friends easily. But I had attracted a bully.

Like a fly round dung balls, Julie made my life slightly more hellish than the Dead did. Mrs Berry had some very choice things to say about Julie and her personal hygiene which did make me feel better, at least I wasn't the only one who thought she was a hag from Hell.

Julie had very blonde hair with a texture like steel wool. She had broad shoulders like an Olympic swimmer, which in fact she grew up to be. She divided her waking hours. For most of the time she was chugging up and down the pool in town. I imagined she cut through the water like a shark, her elbows sticking up like dorsal fins as she crawled through the water. When she was on dry land, as a little light relief from the rigours of Olympian athleticism, she tortured me.

To write it down it seems petty; poking me in the back with a pencil, dropping pencil shavings down my neck, tripping me, letting doors go in my face, name calling. The name calling was particularly pathetic, without much range. 'Bag', 'Slag', 'Hag', 'Nag', the Dr Seuss school of intimidation. But mental torture is always so much meaner. There were the whispering campaigns and the fact that if you stood too near me at breaktime you'd get punched too. No one could afford to be my friend unless they had studied martial arts.

I decided to save up and have karate lessons. I spent evenings dreaming of the day I'd be a black belt and whack Julie on her slightly fuzzy-haired chin with the side of my foot. I didn't want to save up for a gun. No. Firearms would be cheating. I wanted the pure physical pleasure of my own strength and skill. Contact killing.

As it turned out I didn't have to save up for any karate lessons at all. As it turned out, Hal came to my rescue.

We were on the maths corridor. It was like a giant cardboard box, the classrooms partitioned with pre-fabricated flimsiness, small rectangular windows at the tops of the walls which let minimum light and air into the short corridor. There were stairs at one end, doors which trapped fingers. It was nightmarishly easy to be trapped into a corner by a practised bully.

I was shoved into the wall, into the corner. I could smell her breath, oniony, and the smell from her clothes was sharp with a back note of chlorine. She was laughing, a low piggish snorting under her breath, and simply shoving me. Every time someone moved past us she shoved against me as if she was being forced to do so by other people pushing past her.

'Oops…soh-ri,' she said, cartoon-like. 'Oops…soh-ri,' laughing all the time. A couple of girls passed by on their way to the stairs and once again, she shoved right into me, so hard in fact that she nearly lost her balance, and in grabbing at me to steady herself she tipped my balance. I stumbled, fell to the floor.

And then Hal saw his chance, stepped in and took over.

It felt like your arm going dead. When you wake up in the middle of the night and you've been sleeping on your folded arm and all the circulation is gone. You look down at the hand and the arm and it's like it isn't yours. You can't move it but it is still attached to your body.

My whole body felt like that. I couldn't move. Not my eyeballs, not anything. It was as if I'd disappeared. Hal's voice came out of my mouth. It was a torrent of abuse aimed at the person who'd killed him, I think. This afternoon it was aimed at Julie. She just got in the way that day. Afterwards I could only remember pieces of it. He didn't name names, either.

See what I mean? Tell me something important. Give me information.

'Fucking bastard. You shitty piece of shit. You're shit and you touch her. You can't get rid of me. NO. NO. Can't get shut of me you shitey bastard fucker.'

This is shocking enough I know, simply to read cold and black in print on this page. Imagine hearing it. A gruff, male, northern voice, deep and smoky sounding spitting forth from the mouth of an eleven-year-old girl. Let's remember that this was 1970 something and nothing, and I was wearing a white school blouse and a Marks and Spencer regulation box-pleated skirt. I had on a V-neck grey jumper. I was wearing knee socks, for pity's sake.

Suffice to say I was taken to the medical room and Julie never really recovered from the experience.

She never bullied me again. Now she'd seen magic. The chief reason that many people don't believe in magic is terror. It is wild and uncontrollable. It is not a card trick.

I lay on the couch in the medical room feeling pins and needles all over and aching in every muscle I possessed. No pun intended. My Mother had been called away from work and was discussing me in the headmaster's office. I felt strangely calm lying there. It was quiet in the medical room and there was a velux window in the sloping roof so I had a view of the sky, and a silver birch tree that grew just outside in the courtyard off the science labs. It was one of the best days I ever spent in school. Lounging on a sofa in the medical room.

I was a social pariah after that, of course. Which made life a lot easier. Thanks Hal.

Later My Mother came and took me home. She let me lie on the sofa at home and I was fed copious quantities of hot tea and given a cold flannel for my head. My Mother asked a lot of questions that day and I confessed everything. Even about Aunt Mag and the home-made ouija board. That went down like a lead balloon.

Mr Bentley found that his Thursdays were rudely interrupted.

Aunt Mag's racehorse fund was abruptly stopped and the monies in the fund were transferred into premium bonds in my name. My Mother had a big row with Aunt Mag over the ouija board and 'meddling' and 'dabbling' were words that were used quite a lot.

Aunt Mag was at once contrite and terrified. She thought I was possessed and didn't want me in her house. My Mother was thankful; the understairs cupboard was almost full of soap by now. She had a good way to finish the relationship.

She was anxious to do this because she had recently met Mr Dauntsey who worked at the supermarket. He was Fruit Manager and managed to slip us at least three melons a week plus a variety of sub-standard spoiled-in-transit apples, pears and bananas. He looked like a wolf with odd grey-blue eyes under thickish greyish brows. But he didn't scare me. By then nothing scared me. I was becoming fearless.

Mr Dauntsey. Wolf. I remember it now as always being a full moon but that is probably embroidery. When Mr Dauntsey was visiting he did not mind me being in the house. I was quiet and out of the way in my room whilst he and My Mother were ensconced in her 'boudoir'. That's what she always called it, even when we moved house and her allotted space was little more than a box room. My Mother made her living space a boudoir, richer, fuller, lush. She was a bower bird. Making it home.

I don't know how it began. I was doing some homework. I had some music on. David Essex. I was accustomed to the slight noises that would leak out from the boudoir. The odd bump, the slide of an elbow against the wall, the rhythmic headboard drumming. (Turned my music up louder at this point. Bought headphones later. Bliss.)

The noise changed. It was a wafer-thin change, an extra bump.

Another bump. A sharp word, muffled. I stood up then. My ears straining out for sound although I didn't think to switch the music off. I moved onto the landing.

The boudoir was one room down, we had a big house then, four bedrooms and a couple of bathrooms. I moved along the landing, hearing more of the thuds. Not the regular rhythm at all. Arrhythmia. The arrhythmia of someone beating someone else. The arrhythmia of my heart. Now in my mouth.

I could hear his voice now and the sound his fists made on My Mother's flesh. The *chock* sound her head made on contact with the wall.

I pushed open the door. He was naked. Like a wolf with a snake of thick dark hair down his back and thicker curlier hair down his arms. My Mother was underneath him, his hand on the back of her neck, as he held her the way someone holds a puppy they are about to drown. He looked at me with fury. I flew that night. I lifted off vertically and I moved through the air to land on that hairy, animal back.

The impact shoved him forward and he was half crushing My Mother, who was now semi-conscious and bleeding from the mouth, a loosened tooth smearing a trail of blood across the sheeting. He whirled, lashing out at me. His weight shifted from My Mother and in a daze she rolled off the bed, bumping onto the floor at the side. I thought she was dead then and I was going to kill him.

I didn't need to. Rounding on me, catching me round the neck with his hairy arm he thwacked me to the ground. He was punching at me, my head banging on the floor, feeling the static charge from the nylon carpet. I could hear My Mother being sick. The scent of vomit now. Which is when Hal took over. My arms and legs were rigid, rubbery, and his voice spat out of my mouth. Dark, smoky, Northern.

'Fucking bastard. You shitty piece of shit. You're shit and you touch her. You can't get rid of me. NO. NO. Can't get shut of me you shitey bastard fucker.'

Mum's Eye View:
sideways on

Don't mention him. How to see yourself as a complete failure in one easy lesson.

I didn't save her from bloody Mag. I could have brained Mag. But I was more furious at myself. I was so busy having my good time with Jeff Bentley I didn't see it. I didn't bother to look, just cast the kid aside for some pleasures. Your children are a piece of you, like pinching off a bit of dough, it goes on, it makes other loaves or pie crusts but it starts with you. It got so that I couldn't look at Jeff without thinking about Annie. So I broke that off. Punishing myself.

Don't mention Dauntsey. There are things that you just don't let your children see. Your worry. Yourself in bed with your lover. And of course for her to come in like that, with a dead man's voice and the language…How do you feel about that? You feel sick and afraid and powerless. She saved me. What if she'd not? What if that bloke hadn't come through her like that? What if she'd slept in her bed and the next time she'd seen me I'd been giving her a message, make sure your Aunt Mag never finds out they found her in a string bag in the doorway of the chippy.

I was dangerous. I wasn't fit to be let out. I don't know who I was more afraid of. Me. Her.

And you puzzle it out, you know. How all this happened, how you got yourself where you are. The back of my mind was always telling me that I couldn't give up being me, but it also kept telling me that she was always giving up being her.

She didn't have a lot to say for herself. They had a lot to say for her. Through her. I should have found out things. Made enquiries about that Hal bloke for a start. Exorcised him somehow. But I was scared to. Scared of what we might let loose. There weren't demons in her. But there was a demon in me, a little wily git who kept me afraid and stopped me doing what I should.

I never could ask how it felt, if she minded. I was lost on it. What could I do?

Dauntsey never got over it. He got religion shortly after. Which I don't know if I'm pleased about.

So, anyway

We got shut of Mr Dauntsey. We didn't shop at that supermarket any more. Shortly afterwards My Mother got a new job and we moved house. To the other side of town up near Old Park. Big. Victorian. Haunted of course, but I kept that, kept them, from My Mother.

At the time I felt safe. I thought My Mother had moved house because of Mr Dauntsey. That she was cocooning us, making us safe. Now I think back and I am sad to realise that in all reality she was probably just afraid of me. If she could have moved house without me maybe she would. The Hal incidents shook her up. If I had been her, I would have taken me to the library and tried to find out who Hal was and what had happened to him. To try and put things straight.

But I would have done that because I am not My Mother. You can talk to the Dead but you can never really know what another person is thinking.

School. Yes. Well. I considered my time there as akin to being in prison for a crime I had not committed. Apart from being a social pariah and getting on with my homework, I managed a few school discos. Even with my reputation as the class weirdo there were fumbled kisses and slow dancing but most of those early sexual experiences ended badly with my heart broken. It struck me that boys didn't have a thought in their heads. Their genitalia like compasses, always pointing north.

Funny how the words for the male member all smack of stupidity. 'Member' for a start off, some idiot politician. John Thomas, who no doubt plays a banjo in Tennessee. Todger, the thick dog who can never find where you've thrown the stick. Dick, the man who wears the most hideous golf sweaters at the local links. Cock, a strutting brainless bird puffed up with his own importance and getting round *all* the birds. Donger, a dwarf breed of conger eel. Prick, so quick you hardly notice and before you turn your head it's all over.

I did fall in love, usually with desperately unattainable people. The lad in the dry cleaners, the man in the record library. Sean Connery.

What was My Mother's job? For a living she ran the office in a plant hire firm. For a vocation she helped people. That's why we always had more bedrooms, for all the people who would come to stay. Miss Chatham the librarian after her affair with the Head of Libraries. Chris Baker after her husband died and she was scared to go back to her house. He came to see where she was, that was his only unfinished business. There was Ellen Danby, Mrs McCann, Jane Kirkpatrick and her three kids, another French student who burned all our pans. The Hungarian chess team.

She fostered people. She gave them money and comfort. She never expected anything back. She did not mind all the people in her life. In our life.

Which brings me to My Father. He was not located on any map, local or otherwise. What she told me about him was chiefly fairy stories—the most handsome man, the best dancer, the brainiest professor type of thing. Professor of what she could never make her mind up, one time it would be professor of physics, another time he'd have a more artistic bent, doctoring with philosophy. He was Phallus, the Great Greek Hero poncing through my imagination, raising golden trophies and fighting glorious causes but never reading bedtime stories or picking me up from school on a rainy Thursday.

At first I had thought that she said this to protect me, that probably he had been another sad Mr Dauntsey type with cheesy feet and a liking for cold ham sandwiches. I wanted him to be the hero that she so clearly wanted. That she needed.

In the end I realised that the even sadder truth was that she probably couldn't remember who My Father was. I had been conceived on a pile of coats in the back bedroom of someone's semi after too many glasses of English table wine. Doubtless in My Mother's memory My Father was an odd blurred identikit face formed from his own features and the faces in the posters on that back bedroom wall. Steve McQueen. Paul Newman.

He was the first person I looked for. My Father.

I always expected to see him any day now, trundling into my consciousness in a natty chocolate brown suit. He was like a huge surprise, a special secret. I spent years disappointing the Dead because I was looking for him. 'What? You're not My Father? Listen, if it's about Crown Derby I don't want to know.'

My Mother had relationships with all the lorry drivers at the plant hire firm at one time or another. The only person she did not have an affair with was Mr Ringley the regional manager because he had a wife and kids. At least he had a photo of a wife and some kids on his desk. He never talked about them. She asked him once about them, just making small talk as they pored over a map of the local area, sticking pins in the locations of their current rolling stock of vibrating pokers and jib units. Mr Ringley did not talk about his family in office hours.

'They are for home use only,' was his comment. My Mother never told, you know, that she'd seen the family photograph in an old Grattan catalogue. A woman and two kids all kitted out, smiling. Mail order family.

The real pain in the backside was Aunt Mag. Aunt Mag wore a chocolate brown A-line skirt and a too-tight sweater. Every sweater ever invented was too small for Aunt Mag. She had the most enormous bosom. It was like a couple of badgers slung round her neck. Her hips were narrow beneath, stunted in the shade.

I imagine the more gruesome amongst you would like to know how she died. Quickly. She was much older than My Mother, the eldest sister in fact, and she had smoked like a factory chimney since she was twelve. There had been a brief period when she lived in Blackpool as the sidekick to a comedian. Then she had smoked cigars to try and be showbizzy.

One afternoon she was visiting us, we had just had lunch, tinned crab and a green salad with some crispy spring onions and pickled beetroot. I was in the kitchen doing the washing up and My Mother had just nipped over the road for a moment to give a spare key back to one of the neighbours. Aunt Mag was watching television in the front room.

And then she wasn't. She was standing next to me in her chocolate brown sweater and skirt and looking very put out.

'I'm very put out,' she said. She looked familiar of course, because she was Aunt Mag. The chocolate brown wardrobe was also familiar and it took me three tea plates and a cut-glass fruit bowl before I realised. What surprises me looking back is that I didn't panic. I didn't shout or yell or break down in tears. I dried the dishes. I simply looked at her and I thought, 'Oh dear.'

'Are you listening to me? I still had things to do. This is really unfair. Who's going to let the cat in?'

See what I mean about the useless, the futile and the utterly bloody pointless? No one was going to let the cat in. Paul Howarth had just run over it in his Austin Maxi. Not that we knew it at that moment.

'I'm more bothered about Mum. Is there something you want to say to her? If there is, can I just head her off at the pass, because you'll have left yourself in the front room. Can I do that? Save her the shock, eh?'

Aunt Mag's earthly remnants were sitting in the chair, the *TV Times* in one hand. As I was looking at her thinking what needed to be done, My Mother came in behind me. She wasn't hysterical either. She was very quiet then. She looked at Aunt Mag and then at me. Then she phoned the doctor and the undertaker and her other sisters. She seemed to get paler and smaller as the afternoon wore on, until she looked like a storybook representation of a ghost herself. She sat on the stairs until the undertaker came. Then she stood in the kitchen. She made a pot of tea which she didn't drink.

'What was it you wanted to say?' I asked Aunt Mag.

'I want to tell her the truth about Our Dad,' Aunt Mag said, 'I never have got round to it.' She was tugging at the sweater, patting her hair. She always did that, patted it into place even though it was fixed with industrial-strength hair lacquer. She had hair like candy floss, my Aunt Mag.

'What is it?'

'He wasn't who she thought he was is all.'

Warning bells were already clanging in my head.

'What do you mean by that? He wasn't a civil servant, he was a juggler? A transvestite?'

Aunt Mag pursed her lips.

'He wasn't her dad.'

Hurtful. Interfering.

'Aunt Mag, you had fifty-eight years to tell her that.'

'Yes well…You know what it's like.'

'You're not here to deal with it.'

Aunt Mag was patting her hair again, smulching her lips together as if she was smoothing her lipstick.

'She's got a right to know. It was wrong of me not to tell her.'

'I'm not telling her.'

Aunt Mag tried to pull rank then. I walked away. She followed me of course. My Mother was pulling on a coat, ready to go to the register office.

'Strike while the iron's hot,' she said, almost in a whisper. And then My Mother was crying. Sitting on the stairs and heaving out great sobs. Hot, burning tears, all the afternoon's grief sluicing out. I sat with her, held her. Glared at Aunt Mag.

'Tell her now. Strike while the iron's hot like she says. It's got to be done.'

I ignored her. We went out to the register office. When we got back she was still waiting. I kept ignoring her. Until bedtime.

She wouldn't let me sleep.

'I'm not going anywhere until you tell her.'

I was panicking a bit. I did not want to spend the rest of my life with my Aunt Mag nagging at my heels and there was no way on God's green earth that I was going to tell My Mother that her dad wasn't her dad. I knew how that felt. I was so angry with Aunt Mag for wanting to do this. To be so discontented as to want to sow such destruction for someone she had supposedly loved. I couldn't think of a way out. I lay there in the dark with her sitting by my bed, her arms folded defiantly under her badger bosom. It was stalemate for about two days.

Day Three: I had a brainwave. I was about to go out. Pulling on my coat, I kept the most serious face I could.

'Aunt Mag…I think that to clear up all your unfinished business we should tell My Mother about her dad.'

She was patting her hair again now. Her show of triumph.

'But I think we should also tell her about you and Mr Bentley.'

She stopped patting her hair.

'What about me and Mr Bentley?' she looked at me, quizzical. Worried.

'Tuesdays.'

She looked at me for a long moment, her brain whirring all the information. How did I know about that, she was desperate to ask.

'You never saw us. You don't know anything.'

'Mr Bentley told me.'

Aunt Mag looked puzzled.

'He told you. But you were only…oh no…you mean…'

Mr Bentley in his chocolate brown salesman's suit. Only six weeks before. He had loved My Mother, more than all that soap.

When I returned from town Aunt Mag was gone.

I left school and got a job at the plant hire firm with My Mother. I was the cabin boy, there to run a lot of errands and do odd jobs that no one else was being paid to do or could be arsed doing. I didn't mind it. It didn't last.

I got on well with the drivers. I often had to make coffees, do a sandwich run, fetch pasties or pies. I don't know if I was pretty, it never occurred to me, but they all chatted with me. I gave good directions, drew little maps of various towns and their ring roads for people. I was quite good if anyone had to go to Blackpool since we had visited there quite a lot while my Aunt Mag was a comedian's straight man.

My favourite was Beck. I never did know what his first name was. He was always Beck. He had a funny moustache and he was always asking me about where he should take his girlfriend, Shell. Should he book the little Italian place or should they risk the Chinese? He gave her flowers, asking me which I'd like to receive if someone was giving me a bouquet. Asked my advice about buying birthday and Christmas presents. A silver locket, an ankle bracelet. Beck would come in and he would make me some tea and he would always ask if I could give him a hand with his paperwork. This was partly because he liked me but mostly because he couldn't read or write very well. Some people are just meant to be with you.

You know where this is going don't you?

What I remembered was opening the file drawer to look for the Prescotts invoice. A pink invoice. What two of the drivers and one of the admin assistants remembered was seeing me go rigid as a plank and then hearing Beck's voice.

'Love you, Love.'

When I came round I was lying on the couch in Mr Ringley's office and My Mother was sitting on a plastic chair by the door. Back then I thought she was guarding the door. Keeping me safe. Now I look back and I think she was sitting by the emergency exit. Ready to run.

The news was in by then. I could tell by the missing radio. Instead of tinny pop music there was nothing. Silence. I thought then that I should find out where Shell lived and give her the message.

'Where does Shell live?' was all I said.

'Leave it, love.'

My Mother was sitting on the chair like someone waiting for root canal work or the Queen. I opened my mouth to speak and she winced, waiting for someone else's voice to come out. Then she came to me. Took my hand. Squeezed it.

'Leave it, love. She doesn't need it. She needs to start letting go.'

She kissed my hand.

'Leave it, love.'

I was let go myself shortly afterwards. I did quit. I had used company time and paper to type out a neat letter of resignation. I handed it to Mr Ringley. He took it as if it had come straight from the Angel of Death. He looked as if he wouldn't open it in case it was bad news. I prompted him, let him know the contents.

Turned out he was going to drop me anyway. I had saved him the task.

My Mother was waiting for a lift home. We shared a clapped-out car. She knew I'd been let go, not that I had quit.

'Let's go to Valerie's for a brew shall we?'

And she drove us into town. Her driving terrified me. She drove like she was on the dodgems.

Valerie's was a stripped-pine sort of place that we had been going to since I was little. I had progressed from still orange to a pot of tea and seen all the changes of tables and tablecloths. If we went out with Aunt Mag we always had to go to a horrible dark green place called the Chump Chop because they had a smokers' corner. Valerie's always had fresh flowers on every table and cheese on toast available all day. Whatever you asked for you could have. I thought she should have the menus printed up saying simply, 'What do you fancy then love?'

My Mother and I nursed a pot of tea for two and My Mother ate a scone. We didn't talk. We didn't need to. That was one of the best things about her. Understanding silences.

After that I moved away. Not far. Just to the university town up the dual carriageway. I got a small house with a small garden and a job in the archaeology department doing the administration and volunteering for the digs.

I was utterly at home there amongst the bones and the artefacts. The unfinished business there was beyond my talents. Some of the things I wrote down phonetically to try and make sense. English can be a foreign language if the person you are talking to is two thousand years old.

Mum's Eye View:
sideways on

Yes. I was disappointed that Mag didn't have anything to say. I thought she might have some parting shot. I also think that Annie was covering it up. I thought it had to be pretty bad for her not to tell me. To protect me. But I don't know. It was funny between Annie and Mag after the whole Thursdays business.

She's right. There were too many people in the house. I don't know. Couldn't help myself. Had to help them. Even if it was just a roof over their heads for a few weeks. I know I have to be honest here. They protected me from Annie. It didn't have to be so intense if there was a load of us in the house. I didn't have to think all the time about what might be happening in Annie's head, because I had to get a casserole on or hoover the landing.

Don't get me wrong though, I enjoyed helping out. I don't think it did us any harm to link up with so many people. We had a lot of experiences. When Janey Kirkpatrick rolled up with her kids that was a good time for Annie. She had brothers and sisters for a while, like an extended family. I liked to see someone come in through my doorway looking lost or abandoned and then see them three weeks later with their stockinged feet on the coffee table or mowing my lawn. Making themselves at Home.

I know what I did wrong. I'm not perfect.

Onwards

BE WARNED. It starts to get a bit Love Story now. Without the terminal illness I might add.

I had not bothered much with anyone. I'd been taken out to the pictures by a few blokes and had a few dinners. I'd even managed to have sex, but quite frankly they bored me. I couldn't see the point of going out with someone that you didn't really like and trying to make yourself like them.

Most of the young men, and a couple of the older ones I picked out, seemed only interested in one thing. They made small talk, ate dinner or pretended to listen to your boring recollections from your day at work because they felt that this would work some miracle on the elastic of your knickers. They didn't want you. They wanted sex. Conversation was just some boring form-filling requirement that had to be gone through to get to the sex. No one seemed any good at it either. Possibly I wasn't. I wasn't experienced, I hadn't read any books and despite her encyclopaedic knowledge My Mother never told me a thing. She didn't even fill me in on the mechanics of it.

I knew only the most basic stuff, information gleaned from some absurd line-drawing cartoons that we were shown as part of our sex education class at Petri Dish High. These were the cartoons they showed right before they showed us the full colour close-up pictures of penises pus-filled with gonorrhea or todgers dripping with evil venom from some other hideous disease that was 'sexually transmitted'.

It was like aversion therapy really. Except that the only aversion it created in us was to those Czechoslovakian arthouse animated films which are full of simplistic line drawings and philosophical meaning.

For a brief time at the university I was known as the Ice Maiden because I was notoriously hard work on a date. Then I discovered the Ice Maiden Sweepstake. The bet was on as to who could crack the Ice Maiden. 'Crack'. It was their word. I would have preferred 'thaw': you melt the ice with the heat of your passion. But no. They would have a 'crack' at it. Chiselling. Bashing. Clumsy and hurtful. They were no different from the schoolboys really, with their heat-seeking penises.

It took Evan to change that. Evan Bees. He sounds like he should be in a crossword puzzle, which is in fact the first thing I ever said to him. He joined the archaeology department on a research scholarship and he was nearly thirty, that is to say, seven years older than me. He already had a doctorate and somehow that drew me. I blame My Mother entirely, as you do. It was all those fairy stories she had told me about My Dad, the naughty professor.

I don't know that My Mother ever really approved of him. I suppose he just wasn't her type, if that was possible. My Mother had very Catholic taste (ask Father Tansy). There was one day I remember, when we had decided to tackle her back garden. It had become a wilderness, so tangled with brambles that getting from the back gate to the back door was like a scene from *Sleeping Beauty*. She thought it was a site of outstanding natural beauty, but her neighbour had complained.

Evan picked his way through the brambles, unwilling to secateur them because they were going to fruit, the small green baubles waiting to bask in the sun. There was a moment, a look that passed between them, as if in saying this he had somehow passed a test for her. I watched him, the sappy green scents around us, the bitter sting of the nettles, as he tied knots into the twine, squinting into the sun as he tied them to the fence. We made blackberry jam a few weeks later, none of which we shared with the neighbour.

When we were working together it always felt as if we were uncovering treasure. He thought the bodies were travellers in time. Evan always seemed so connected to the earthly remains, as if he didn't have veins and arteries, instead he had ley lines. As if he picked up energy, was tuned to the earth, and I was tuned to Heaven.

Well, I did warn you.

And I claimed the money on the Ice Maiden Sweepstake too. 'Evan Bees is the winner of the Ice Maiden Sweepstake', I pinned on the notice board. Sent it round as a memo and signed my name. Evan had no clue what that was about. Another reason I loved him. I found the cheque for £150 in my pigeon hole on the Friday. There was some of my Aunt Mag in me.

I think it is apt that people say, 'I fell in love'. It is exactly like that. One minute you're fine. You're rational. The next you're reeling on the floor semi-concussed wondering what it is that has poisoned your heart so.

I couldn't be without him. We spent hours in the department together, cataloguing newly excavated skeletons. If I had had any sense I would have thought this was not really the most auspicious beginning to a love story. It smacked more of a murder mystery. But I didn't have sense. I had fallen in love and was not right in the head.

Funny to look back. I don't look at the photos. Not that there are many. There is only one of him. We had had a walk up to Long Way Crop, taking a picnic of sausage rolls and crisps. It was freezing cold that day but we didn't care. The weather meant that it would be just us up there. With our greasy sausage-rolled kisses. At least, Evan thought we would be alone because, naturally, he couldn't see the cohort of Roman soldiers busy finishing the road that ran along the ridge. The beginning and the end all in a few yards of each other.

I didn't usually carry a camera. It was just in the bottom of the bag. We'd been out at a dig earlier in the week and the chap in charge had got a notion about using instamatic cameras to take instant images of the site and the finds. I was rummaging for a tissue and pulled out the camera. I was laughing at a scrunched and unintentional polaroid it had taken of the inside of my bag. I looked up at Evan. He was looking out across the view. He was miles away. I wanted to bring him back. To keep him.

There are just a few shards to be picked over. Catalogued. I wonder who that girl is, because she isn't me.

Anyway, whatever I was like back then I was liked by Evan Bees. He understood silences too. He had a sense of history as acute as my own and he'd say things like, 'I wonder what the last person to touch this was thinking,' as we pored over the curved handle of a long-ago-disintegrated bucket. We looked at earrings and brooches and thought of the people who had pinned up their clothing against the wind, or whether the earrings had been a love token. What amazed me was that sometimes we hadn't been speaking but we knew what each was thinking.

Yeah. Right.

No one bothered to let me know. Drop me a hint. We had a huge church wedding in a massive cathedral crammed to the rafters with history. Not a word. The bastards.

We did not have children. We had fun trying. Or I thought so. I'm a medium after all, not a mind reader. We seemed to be trundling along very nicely. I suppose the clues were there, he was always so serious and intense. Especially in bed. It was as if he wanted to savour every last moment. As if every day was his last. As if he was a soldier heading off, uncertain, to a war.

First hint I got was when he didn't come home one evening in December. I waited. I waited. I waited.

I panicked. I thought of Beck and Shell. Which made me stop panicking. If he was dead he would come to tell me so. It would be his unfinished business. He hadn't turned up. He was safe.

I waited. I waited. I waited. I waited. I waited. Christmas came and I waited, waited up like a kid waiting for Father Christmas.

Neither of them showed up. He could have got a lift back on that sleigh you know. If he'd tried. They could have both come tumbling down that chimney.

They found his car abandoned by a tourist information office in Northamptonshire. The keys were still in it. I drove it home. I parked it in the drive and after about a year I drove it to the nearest dealership and left it on the forecourt with the documents and the keys in it.

Those keys, glinting and chinkling like a lure for Sam.

Mum's Eye View:
sideways on

She found school difficult. High school. But then who doesn't find school difficult? It's all hectic competition. Competition for good marks. Competition for sports teams. Competition for boys. She didn't have the usual teenage rampage which isn't surprising considering all that was going on in her head. Well, no, not in her head. That makes it sound like mental illness which it isn't. Wasn't. I thought…suspected…Had her checked out. They did these tests. Nothing invasive, a bit of a chat with the psychiatrist and some putting wooden blocks in holes…or was that when she was a baby?

Anyway they couldn't find anything wrong with her, which left me at a bit of a loss. No one really believes in mediums do they? I know there was our Sidney, but that was a long time ago and he was more of a showman than anything. A parlour trick. People believed in it then. They even had Conan Doyle going didn't they?

What my girl said was different. I had a lot of documentary evidence. There wasn't just Mrs Berry, whatever she's told you… She has told you hasn't she?…When she was really little, just tootling around in the pushchair, she could talk a lot. Very advanced.

One health visitor said to me, 'She's been here before.' Which I thought…I ought to have thought…was creepy. But if I'm honest, I agreed. The first time I agreed with any of them. A battalion of spinsters eager to tell you what the books say but without any 'hands on' experience. But this woman. Just came right out and said it. And I was dishonest then. I didn't tell her that only that week my girl had been sitting in the pushchair as we walked past the carpark where The Bind used to be…

You don't know The Bind?…slums they were. Cottages. Set

up by Sir Charles Whitworth's grandfather and left to go to rack and ruin. I remember when I was a girl running round them all full of holes, windows falling out and floors caving in. They got shut of them in the fifties. Floored the lot. Then they couldn't decide what to do and the weeds grew and then finally they made it into a carpark.

My girl had never seen The Bind but that day she's in the pushchair and she points and she says, 'When I lived here before I lived in The Bind…but you won't remember because you weren't my mammy then…' serious as you like. 'When I lived here before…' she'd say it every time we went out. And then she didn't anymore.

I wasn't relieved either when she ended up at the uni and met Evan. He was too…and I know you'll say that this is with hindsight and you're always wiser looking back…but seriously, he was too good looking. You wanted to crack his nose.

I believed they could be happy. With my girl you believed more in fate or destiny, that maybe here was the other half of herself, they got on that well. In fact sometimes they were a bit spooky. Like the Midwich Cuckoos. Have you read that book? Or maybe you've seen the film…all the little blonde kids? Not that she's blonde.

I'm not kidding though. If I ever find Evan Bees and he isn't dead, I'll kill him.

Seven years.
January, the first

SEEMED TO last the whole year. It was cold and the world seemed dark as if it would never get light again. I woke up day after day to endless grey cloud that never lifted. I seemed to repeat the same day over again. Me getting up. Me seeing grey sky. Me getting on with the washing/toilet cleaning/biscuit eating. Me hurrying to the door every time anyone put a leaflet through or delivered a paper. Me scaring them as I tore open the door, hoping that it was Evan.

I ate to sustain myself. If the Bourbon biscuit hadn't been invented and sold in huge bulk packs, I would have starved.

Me waiting until midnight before I locked the doors. Me waking every hour, almost on the hour, because I thought I heard the gate squeak, or a familiar voice in the street, or his foot on the stair.

I didn't get messages then. I didn't go anywhere. The only member of the chocolate-brown-clad brigade I saw was a man who was buried in the concrete foundations of the supermarket. He was stupid and pointless too. All he cared about was revenge. His message was always, 'Tell Eddie he's dead meat.' I wondered who was waiting for him, who was existing on sugar products until he came home.

He accosted me in the Bourbon biscuit aisle, directly above his concrete grave I suppose. Anyway, there I am hurrying to stack my trolley with supplies of chocolate brown biscuits so that I can get home to find that my wandering husband has returned. Up pops Concrete Man.

'Hey. You.' I looked up. Spotted the chocolate brown outfit. Bourbon biscuit brown. He had on a polo neck sweater that made him look porky and a leather jacket that I imagined had been chocolate brown suede even before he died. 'Tell Eddie he's dead meat.'

At first I tried to make an effort. I asked about Eddie and his possible whereabouts. I admitted that I didn't know Eddie and would need this information to give him the message. Concrete Man seemed to think I was being obstructive. Why didn't I know Eddie? Oh right, I was one of Eddie's mates...

I didn't listen. I didn't care. I whizzed away down the aisle only too certain that when I arrived home Evan would already be there with a smile and a cup of tea.

Which of course he wasn't. And there came the day when Concrete Man asked me to tell Eddie and I simply said, 'I told him.'

Eddie wasn't too pleased, and accosted me by the doors about three weeks later. 'Why didn't you warn me?'

I kept pushing my trolley. Eddie was in a chocolate brown T-shirt and chocolate brown underpants, clearly an outfit that he wore to bed. He also had a chocolate brown bloodstain seeping out of his chest. He was deeply scary. In his fury he set an entire rack of trolleys rolling into the carpark after me. A huge metallic silver snake of trolleys, their wheels hissing across the tarmac.

I wanted a messenger. I wanted someone that I could turn to and say, 'Ask Evan if he's dead. Tell me he isn't dead. Tell me something, tell me anything.' But there was no one.

You might ask what My Mother was doing at this time. You might have completely forgotten her existence. I almost had. She tried to 'bring me out of myself', as she put it, but I was a hard taskmaster. I made no effort at all. I didn't need to be brought out. She didn't seem to understand that the only thing that was going to put me right was Evan Bees arriving on the doorstep.

My Mother worried and was powerless.

'You can't stop your life like this,' she said, concerned, eating her way through a chicken and mushroom pie she had brought over. Then she uttered the magic words.

'What are you going to do if he never comes back?' She was ultra-serious, teary even. She attempted to stroke my hair, the way she had when I was little.

I could be coy about this and say, 'I don't remember, but I think I hit her…' But that would be more than coy, that would be a lie. I walloped her, a great lashing blow that caught the edge of the pie and made it look as if her head had exploded and was bleeding chicken and mushroom in cream sauce.

Fair play to the woman. She picked the dish off the floor, got a tea towel for her hair, and after a quick, 'I'll see you tomorrow,' she headed off.

February, the second

T HE FOLLOWING February I had been quite ill. A diet consisting entirely of Bourbon biscuits is not good for you. I was picking up now on a diet of lemon risotto and herb chicken. This was food I could shove in the oven. I could cook the chicken six or eight pieces at a time on the Monday and still be eating it on the Friday or Saturday.

One Sunday I looked out at the car and its covering of leaves and bird crap and I made a decision. My Mother's 'What if he never comes back?' was still ringing in my head. I was reaching a different stage now. I think there are about seven stages to grief: Bashful, Dopey, Grumpy, Sleepy, Donner, Blitzen and Rudolf. 'What if he never comes back?' had been in my head since the first moment they found his car.

I decided that getting rid of the car was a good idea. I would give it away and, therefore, I wouldn't be haunted by the cash. I knew that if I advertised it and had to choose someone to sell it to I never would. I would simply be left standing in the driveway with a series of eager blokes as I looked for an Evan substitute. If you don't look like Evan, sound like Evan…in fact if you aren't Evan Bees, you cannot have his car.

I asked My Mother to follow in her car for a lift home. I drove it to the dealership out on the industrial estate. I chose it because it had banners flying. It looked medieval somehow, as if any moment Richard the Lionheart would pop out of the office and try and sell you a Daihatsu. I drove it onto the forecourt, parked it out of the way with the keys, the MOT, the road tax and all the documents I could find. Then I walked away.

I kept walking. My Mother locked up her car in the layby and she walked alongside me. We had one of our silences. The most understanding one ever in history. We walked and we kept walking, turning off the road onto the public footpath they had built to skirt the landfill site. The one they landscaped with silver birch trees so that the landfill site was one of the most beautiful places in the whole town.

We kept walking. Out past the reservoir and onto the Roman road, past Long Way Crop until we climbed and climbed steadily to the bare rocks of Redstone Crags.

'He isn't dead,' I said at last. My Mother looked at me again, ultra serious. This time I was braced for what she was going to say.

'How do you know, love?'

'He hasn't told me so.'

She nodded but I could tell by her lips, pursed like prunes, that she wasn't finished.

'Maybe he has nothing to say.' She put her hands into the kangaroo pockets of her jacket then. 'Perhaps he's just all settled.'

She didn't talk to the Dead but my God she could read minds.

The next morning Sam called, from the dealership. He had got my details from the car documents. He was most anxious about it all and determined that he should sell the car and I should have the money.

'Don't need the money,' I said, rather rudely. Not that he cared, he was a car salesman, he dealt routinely with bolshy gits.

'Do you want me to give the money to a charity then? Your favourite...Or your husband's favourite.'

'Give it away. Or raffle it.'

There was a pause then.

'That's spooky Mrs Bees. My sister works at Longcauseway Primary School, they could do with the cash.'

They had a prize draw and raised I don't know how many thousand quid. I was happy. I didn't know where Longcauseway Primary was. I never had to walk past it. I never had to look at it and be forever reminded of the car. Forever reminded of Evan.

Sam fell in love with me, but I felt that I was being unfaithful. I was waiting. I am sorry that I broke Sam's heart, but I did not ask him to fall in love.

Sam knew about the waiting but he thought he would win through in the end. He thought, and I think My Mother aided and abetted him in this, that a year and a half was a long time (I was probably well into the Donner and Blitzen stage of the grief process by then) and that a new relationship was the next step towards a new life. My Mother had some very subtle ways.

'You still see them don't you?' she asked one afternoon about six weeks into Sam's ill-advised courtship.

We were in Valerie's. She had made a fresh batch of rock buns that day. I loved the rock buns at Valerie's. They had lemon zest in them that came from lemons. Tiny curls of peel in the fluffy dough. I don't know where she got her sultanas, she got them from somewhere that managed to dry them with the juice still in.

'Who's them? The Driscolls from next door?...The O'Learys?' I was being particularly obtuse. Helped myself to another rock bun.

'They still talk to you.'

'Yes.'

'You don't tell me about it.'

I couldn't really tell if her tone of voice was intrigued, put out or just plain nosey.

'They don't have anything to say to you.'

'What about Sam? Does he know?'

'You think they'll frighten him off?'

I was not harsh. I was honest. My Mother ordered another pot of tea for two. She let it brew for a long time before she came out with it.

'What did your Aunt Mag say?'

It is to my credit that I didn't spit out rock bun in startlement. I didn't choke or splutter or drop my teacup. More than ever I did not want My Mother to find out her true history. It seemed so wonderful that someone could have a real fairy story, one that they had actually lived. I needed just one real-life fairy story then. My Mother had always provided them.

'Nothing. I suppose she was just all settled.'

My Mother smiled as I handed back her own words of wisdom.

'She didn't say anything...about her birth?'

'Nothing.'

Now my curiosity was aroused. My Mother was bursting to tell me, but felt she shouldn't. She sipped at her tea for a while and looked out of the window, watching a traffic warden write out a ticket for a blue Mercedes.

'They found her you know.'

'Found her? Aunt Mag?'

My Mother nodded.

'Your gran and granddad thought they couldn't have children. Turns out that it was just stress really. They'd got themselves so worked up about it they couldn't relax enough. Actually, I think it's because they didn't know how to have sex, but anyway...One evening they were at the pictures and they came out early because they weren't struck with the picture. I don't know what it was... something with Clark Gable in, I think. Your granddad never did like him. Anyway, they were a bit peckish and thought they'd call in at the chippy. Your Aunt Mag was in the chippy doorway. Wrapped in a blanket in a string bag, hooked round the door handle.'

In the silence that followed this our tea turned cold and the traffic warden called in the tow truck and had the blue Mercedes taken away. As the car was trawled away she spoke.

'They thought she was a gift.'

My Mother was definitely teary now and having to halt her speech so that she wouldn't crack. 'All parcelled up in the chippy doorway. If it wasn't for your Aunt Mag they wouldn't have had me, or Lorna or Marjie...Once they had her, you see, she took their minds off it all.'

See what I mean about My Mother and fairy stories?

Prince Charming. Not Sam and that's for sure, although he tried his hardest. We went out at least twice a week to the pictures, to the huge multiplex they had just then built at the motorway junction.

I don't know what I was doing. I liked the company and I liked to see films. I didn't see how sitting in the dark for two to four hours every week with a man could make him imagine that you were falling in love with him. But of course it can, because as you're sitting there completely engrossed in the film, losing yourself utterly in a non-existent, non-threatening dream world, your companion is sitting in the dark making it up in his head.

He is looking at the light from the screen as it moves across your hair. He is looking at your silhouette as you sit beside him. He is listening to you laugh or watching you sit tense or jump into the air at the thriller. He's making up a fairy story.

If I had been braver. Fairer. Just different.

Then I suppose I would have gone out with him for dinner, or possibly ice-skating, or to the zoo and then he would quickly have realised what a sour old cow I was. He might have noticed that I was sitting in the zoo cafe thinking that perhaps Evan had got a job in the kitchens, somewhere that I couldn't see. Maybe even as we sat there he was mucking out the elephants.

In the cinema I put Evan Bees to the back of my mind. Put him in a little box. One of those dog carrier things. Going to the cinema was not something Evan and I had ever done.

I let Sam into bed, too, which was pure evil. For then we were both making up our own personal fairy stories. I shut my eyes and thought of Evan and Sam opened his eyes and thought of me. Or at least the me that he imagined I was.

I was cruel then, and I should have known it. I knew what it felt like to be used. I remembered that day with Beck and Shell. I should have known better.

I think about Sam sometimes now and I realise that he is walking around with a fake set of memories about our time together. Our time together did not exist. I was not spending it with him.

My Mother had been spending a lot of time with Brian. Brian was a forest ranger at the Goatmill Woodland Park. He wore a green uniform with khaki trousers and big brown boots. He made me think of Little John—he was a tall bloke, broad across the shoulders. He was a fairytale giant I suppose, with his big hands and his big feet only too ready to take care of My Mother.

He was the end of the house guests. She had the Hungarian chess team staying again that year. They were over for a tournament. It is a measure of My Mother that their relationship was so tightly bonded. She had slept with them all at one point or another, solace for a lost match, stress relief for an aching head. Whatever, she had been with all of them. Now when they visited they brought photos of their kids and their wives and talked of their family lives as if My Mother was in some way part of this, had contributed something to their way of living.

Once they were gone Brian was firmly in the picture, standing over to the left a bit and squinting in the dappled forest shade. He was always squinting. He needed glasses.

My Mother imagined that I was with Sam and it was going to be permanent. Or possibly she chose to believe that. She needed Brian after all she'd gone through with me. It only took them three months to decide to get married and before you knew it the big house that had known so many lame ducks and lodgers was up for sale. She and Brian bought a small bungalow on the edge of the Woodland Park because Brian had to be up at the crack of dawn for his forestry work.

This is where she was starting to go quietly batty due to the lack of hangers on. Then she decided to open a tea shop.

The Glade was exactly what the Woodland Park needed. It began as a glorified shed which My Mother bought and painted up. She painted it Fjord Blue, and the window frames white. She put up galvanised troughs that she recycled from a farm sale and planted them up with flowers. She was one of the first in the town to put tables outside.

It was never quiet in there. People came just for the tea and never looked at the Woodland. And her vocation for helping people out shone through in her ragtag-and-bobtail selection of waitresses and assistants.

There was Zara who had been sacked from a hairdressers for selling the hair to an upholstery firm for stuffing. The story was that Zara had high hopes of being trained as a stylist. She was delighted to get the job as trainee at the salon. She didn't mind sweeping up hair occasionally, in fact she considered it part of the training. However after six weeks of nothing else she opted to take her own action. She was selling the hair so she could afford to go to college and study hairdressing. My Mother thought this showed initiative. The happy ending for Zara is that she grew up to be a cafe owner. The cafe chain she owns now has elegant green parasols and patio heaters.

There was Aurora and Lynsey and Gemma. Aurora who was very shy but went on to become the manager. Lynsey who started doing some of the baking and ended up winning a national competition and running a bakery business of her own. She supplied The Glade. She still does. She makes this maple syrup and pecan sponge cake that is cosmic.

But no one makes rock buns like Valerie's.

Mum's Eye View:
sideways on

I love The Glade. And my girls. They've all come on, you know.
I don't know if I see myself in them, the wild and the untamed.

Who am I kidding really? I wasn't wild and untamed. I was
lost and naïve. I needed someone to save me and no one bloody
bothered. I mean, it worked out in the end. Not just my girl, but
Brian.

Brian said a funny thing. He didn't want to know. That's it. He
didn't want to know. Not about Mr Bentley or that Dauntsey
bloke. Not about my girl's father or Patrice or the Hungarian
chess team or ANYONE. He said simply that was the past. It
was all the moments that were gone, not to be revisited and not
available on video to be endlessly played back. I don't even have
a lot of photographs. None really. He said he's just interested in
me, who I am now and what we will do together.

If you made him up, no one would believe you. I look at him
sometimes when he's chopping wood or whatever, and I wonder
how I got him, where he even came from. We live in the forest
and it's like some fairytale and he's the kindly giant.

I always preferred the kindly giant to Prince Charming. There
was always something so drippy about princes to me as a kid. I
loved the Beast and I used to sob my heart out at the end when
he turned into the handsome prince because somehow Beauty'd
lost. I wanted the Beast back. I think it was probably the fact that
they always draw them in the storybooks with those silly periwigs
on. You can't fancy someone with a periwig and satin breeches
on.

But there's something welcoming about a man in a forest with
a spotted handkerchief and a bit of cheese. Don't you think?

March, the third

B Y THE March after that, I lost hope. I simply put it down on the worktop one morning as I turned to the fridge for the milk. I never picked it up again. This was good for me—after all it was now two years since Evan had 'popped out'. However, it was the undoing of me and Sam.

At last I didn't have to use Sam as a cipher for Evan. I broke off the relationship with Sam. He wanted to remain friends. I didn't. I felt that was giving false hope.

Sam stuck with it. We still went to the pictures together. I made it completely clear that I was not going to be in love with him ever. I did. I could have written it out I suppose, signed it, had it witnessed by a notary public.

It was Sam who came to tell me that My Mother was dead.

On the CCTV tape you oversee it. As if you are God and your eyesight isn't too good. You can only see in grainy black and white. That's what a few millennia of gazing down on the deeds of Earth probably does to you. Or should that be You?

You look down powerless and you can see My Mother sitting on a chair next to the suited man. You can see the moment that he begins to sweat. See the sweat darken his armpits on his handmade suit. And My Mother is so calm as she leans to talk to him. I don't hear what she says. You can see almost from the outset that the sweating, suited man isn't going to make it. He's squirming, sweating, a boiler about to explode.

The robbers were the worst kind. Virgin bank robbers fumbling with their weaponry, unsure where to put what.

You see the suited man gripping the metal chair arms fit to bend them as his heart begins to stop. He keels over, slithers from the chair. My Mother is already helping him, cradling his head as he goes so he doesn't concuss himself on the chair frame. She is moving to his side, pulling at his clothes, loosening his tie.

The robbery is by now second fiddle to My Mother. The man nearby is getting edgy, doesn't know whether to watch what they are doing. Or not watch what they are doing because he can see that this man is going to die and he doesn't want to see that. But he's going to be in trouble if they get out of hand. He jabs at My Mother with his gun and says something we can't hear.

My Mother ignores him. She is adjusting the suited man's head so that his airway is clear. She is busy slapping her lips onto the suited man's lips, trying to breathe life into him. The robber jabs her some more. Finally she pushes the gun away and tells him off. Then she turns back to the man and his malfunctioning heart. She turns and she is giving the man mouth-to-mouth resuscitation. The Kiss of Life.

Only the virgin bank robbers have other ideas, and My Mother dies as she lived, kissing a man for all she is worth. The suited man is so taken with her he is swift to follow. The bank robber starts to shriek in panic like a frightened child.

Brian carried My Mother out through the doors afterwards in his giant's arms.

The virgin robbers didn't get the money. They got a murder trial. They were ushered out of a police van with blankets over their heads on their way to the courts. They were stupid. They were pointless. I didn't care about their wives or mothers or sisters.

I remember noticing, as Sam and I sat there, the light from the windows fading as the day drew on, that Sam's hands were shaking. He never stopped shaking and we must have sat there for over five hours.

I wasn't crying. I didn't feel grief. I was simply…waiting. My Mother had been killed that lunchtime in the bank. I didn't seem to believe it. It wasn't really believable, was it? How could this happen? We weren't in a film. It was our ordinary bank on Tonge Street next to the Cheap Trick Shoe Store. My cousin, Karen, worked in the bank on one of the tills. After the robbery she gave up. She cashed in her life savings and travelled the world. Running away, she called it.

But on that day it was Our Bank. On a perfectly normal street with zebra crossings and traffic lights and a woman outside the video store pranging her bumper as she attempted to back into too tight a space. She was dropping off her video. A film titled *Master Key* about a bungled bank robbery.

I tried to remember what My Mother had been wearing that day. Whatever it was it would now be chocolate brown.

My Mother never came back. Maybe because chocolate brown was never a colour that suited her. It washed her out. She suited deep plums and lush aubergines.

I waited. I felt all right. I didn't have any grief, assured in the knowledge that soon she would be back to talk to me, with her unfinished business to be solved. That unfinished business would be the rest of my life. She had my lifetime left to fill with good advice and understanding silences.

My Mother never came back.

I kept The Glade going. Brian only talked to the trees. I finally gave up my job at the university and opted to run The Glade full time. I simply changed allegiance. Instead of waiting forever in the university for Evan to find me I decided to wait for My Mother instead.

She would know where to find me. She had known where to find me at the university. When I worked too late and stayed too long she would roll up in her car and drag me out, drop me home. Now when I worked too late and stayed too long I simply fell asleep where I sat down and woke up the next day with my hair in a pat of butter and a crick in the back of my neck from lying in a draught.

I slept very well at The Glade. Whether I had my hair in a pat of butter or not. I could be propped up against the turquoise-blue tongue and groove panelling or simply slumped over the scrubbed wooden worktop. I rested.

My Mother never came back.

Eventually I realised I would have to change tack and I thought about the room, the little anteroom I often saw when those with unfinished business came to see me. I'd go one night and visit them. I had questions to ask. I had unfinished business.

April, the fourth. April, the first.
Time for wrestling the angel

IT WAS hard to get there. Usually I was an outsider, looking in. I had to will myself into that small space. Not that it was my physical being that got there. That would have been easy. A bottle of pills.

Chucking yourself off the bridge at Endsea had become more difficult of late. The council had employed a man, a former wrestler, to keep an eye out for suicides. He had rescued five people in the first three months of his employment. He didn't talk them down, he dragged them bodily. Then he locked them into the tollbooth next to his office whilst he brewed tea. The local paper wanted to run a story about him being a hero, but he wouldn't have it. He maintained that it wasn't him who saved anyone. It was the tea.

A journalist attempted to cross the bridge and break into his little office and talk with him. He locked her in the tollbooth, out of harm's way.

Out of Harm's Way. The Beast, Harm. With a lick and a promise to do you no good.

The bit of myself that I sent was my astral self. My dream self. And I had to keep myself there. Concentrate hard. It was like sitting an A-level Dreaming paper. As if I had three hours to accomplish this. To get there, argue my case and see My Mother.

I couldn't argue. I had no case. My Mother was dead. The end. But I stayed there.

There were three people there, all with messages. This time I understood why they wanted to say what they did. Why it was important to have that last string attached to the world. But it is a piece of string. As cheap and tatty as that. There is the time and there is the end.

And as I stood, my dreamy astral self, I realised that this really was a waiting room. Just like a dentist's waiting room complete with out-of-date magazines. No one was reading them. And I was in Technicolor. I was quite blinding and odd, most especial-ly to myself. I had to stop thinking about my meaty self, the self lying on my bed supposedly having a nap. Everything I was kept me in that odd little waiting room. It needed plants.

Hal stepped forward. Hal was still visiting me then and he looked very upset to see me there. Not upset that I was dead. Upset that I was dead and would therefore be unable to carry any more of his messages or settle his unfinished business.

'What you doing here?' was his greeting. How typical, you get to Heaven and you expect Hosanna in the slightest. But, of course, I was only in the anteroom.

Who else was there? Can I remember? I remember Hal because he was trying to move into me again and I knew the minute he did that I'd be back in my bedroom shouting obscenities and poor old Sam would come rushing up the stairs.

'I've come to see My Mother.'

'Can't. Not if she isn't here. Doesn't want to see you if she isn't here.'

I was not in any sort of mood to hear, 'Your mother does not want to see you.'

Oh God, now I can remember, Mrs Berry was there. Cutting coupons out of the magazines. She looked over her glasses at me. 'She came through. I told her what I thought, you know, about her cleaning the bath with her cast-off knickers.'

'We don't live there anymore. Go and haunt someone else,' I snapped. And then I approached the door. It had a handle. A brass one. As I touched it Mrs Berry piped up, 'Don't touch that, I've just polished it. You'll get finger marks on it.'

But I touched it anyway. The bland, chocolate brown MDF door. I was determined, pushing it inwards. Which is when I had the tussle with the angel. The door was rammed back at me, only it wouldn't close because, as I had come prepared, I had jammed my astral foot in there. I pushed against the door and the angel pushed back at me. I could see feathers, strong feathers like the ones that fall from a swan. Feathers you could make things with, chieftain headdresses or efficient quill pens.

A muscular arm was reaching down now and it seemed to lengthen immeasurably so that the angel would not have to stoop and lose his/her/its traction on the door. But it wasn't the force of the angel that made me stumble and fall back to my dreaming brain. It was the force of the grief. The force of knowing that now I had to realise that she was not coming back; that she was, indeed, gone.

And how cruel I was. How desperate and thoughtless. My Mother had liked Sam and so I stuck with him. I grieved hard, crying on his shoulder so that mould grew on his smart car-salesman jackets. I moved out of my place, my horrid house that seemed like the gateway to Hell, the house my Evan had vanished from. The house My Mother had popped into that morning on her way to go to Our Bank.

I ran away like the coward I am. The coward I was.

My escape hatch was Sam's house. A cramped little dolly house with chrome furniture that I had no feeling for at all. I hated the kitchen and its yellow cupboard doors. I felt claustrophobic in the bedroom with its white-fitted wardrobes, boxing me into the bed, banging my knees on the wall every morning that I got up. I suffered the bathroom where your elbows knocked against the washbasin when you made to wipe your bum.

It was not Home. It was a Hiding Place. By accident I made Sam happy. A fake happy. A lie, an untruth. A fairy story.

I was the wicked fairy. I cast a spell. Spells break.

I don't know what the change was. It was one of those stages of grief I suppose, my grief for My Mother caught up with my grief for Evan. I was walking home to the dolly house one evening after quite a hard day at The Glade. Sam had offered to pick me up but I enjoyed the walk to Dollyville.

It was quite a shock that afternoon, to be on the phone to Sam and hear his familiar, safe-as-a-castle voice and realise that yes, actually, I had found something that I enjoyed. I could feel pleasure. Immediate twinge of guilt that I could still feel this when really I should be wallowing in desperation. I waited to see if My Mother would come back at that moment to tick me off. She was not a woman to wallow in desperation any day of her life.

So I walked back. It was lighter, heading towards May, official Summer Time. The trees were coming into leaf, buds around, that green whiff that comes with the edge of the frost as it zaps everything into action. We had had a sunny afternoon, chill in the shade but baking and golden in the sunlight. Outside The Glade the weathered wooden tables all smelt fresh and woody, releasing the scents of the two summers they had sat out there. I felt weathered myself under my sweatshirt now, my skin warming as I walked.

There was an avenue leading through the trees from The Glade. It wound round in a slight curl so that although you knew the road to town was there, you couldn't see it. I walked along listening to the birds, a great tit insistent in the treetops. I could hear the squirrels fighting. Once or twice I met a dog and its owner, people escaping from the edges of work, letting themselves free in the forest.

I moved across the gravel of the carpark and out onto the road. I walked along, keeping ahead of the traffic which jammed for the lights at the far junction. I jammed it further when I used the crossing lights.

I walked on, further into town, cutting down now through the Old Mill area of rows of Victorian houses. The kind of two-up, two-down that the estate agents like to call cottages. There were front yards here made into lush gardens, clematis climbing, twining with ivies along rose arches and up obelisks. One or two people had turned their space into a scrap yard, bent prams and motorbikes. There was a gnome haven, hideously coloured.

I kept on until I reached the hornbeam-hedged alleyway that cut through to the allotments on Whitworth Lane. There he was again, Sir Charles, haunting the town he had been so responsible for.

It was as I moved out into the patchwork of blue sheds and black compost bins that I realised I felt at home here. There was an ambitious polytunnel and a greenhouse or two, bamboo canes ready for runner beans, early potatoes, a man digging a trench for his sweet peas, a cast out cottage-style sofa with a coffee table and two old gents sitting in it, drinking tea.

If anyone can be blamed, or named as correspondents, I suppose it might be Mr Jellico and Mr Anstey. They spotted me as I paused behind the chain-link perimeter fence to take in the full view of the Whitworth Lane allotments. I was having a strange moment, whether it was revelation or the muggy afternoon temperature I couldn't tell and didn't care. Either way the sky was filling with prickling black stars and the scent of rich, sweet rot from compost heaps. I reached out for the chain link, reaching through, to try and get in there. To be safe.

Mr Jellico put the kettle on their camping stove as Mr Anstey came to rescue me.

I sat on the sofa, in the warm spot vacated by Mr Jellico. He opened out a deckchair and a parasol as Mr Anstey poured the tea.

'It's a muggy old day...'

'...and a longish walk,' they said. They assimilated me into their world with ease. They talked as if I spent every afternoon sitting on their sofa.

'How's tricks up at The Glade then?' Mr Anstey asked. We chatted then about the day, how a party of old ladies from the bowling club had descended like locusts, emptying the cool cabinet of Genoese fancies and Barm Brack.

'Your mother always made wonderful Barm Brack. Did she use a special brew of tea to soak the fruit?'

Mr Jellico eyed his friend warningly as if I might rant with grief at any moment. Instead I thought of My Mother steeping the sultanas and raisins in a vast bowl filled with tea.

'No. Just Typhoo. Only she always put it into hot tea. She was always too impatient to wait for it to cool.'

Before long we were talking about the mysteries of Valerie's rock buns. When it grew dark they lit camping lanterns and offered cardigans. The kind with latticed leather buttons.

I had a sort of affair with Mr Anstey and Mr Jellico. Instead of heading home to Sam I sat on the sofa with Mr Anstey and Mr Jellico. I relished their easy company, their army tales, their gardening tips. It was my pocket of delight. There were no pockets of delight in Sam's house. Just banged elbows and boxes. The chairs were box shaped. The sofa. The television. Sam even called it The Box. It began to box me in.

I drank some tea. Good tea.

'Where do you live then? You still live at your mum's old place?' Mr Anstey asked one evening.

'Dollyville,' I said without thinking. They knew where I meant.

'Out Barncroft Meadows? Or the other place...'

'Burrow Hills,' I said. The marketing people had a field day thinking up names for Dollyville and Toytown. In recent times, as the toytown developers have spread their houses over the green belt, they have become even more fantastical, as if the cramped little prison camps that they call housing estates are 'villages' or 'rural towns'. They have street names from *Watership Down* or *The Lord of the Rings*. Badger Levels, Bilbo Bend, The Stride.

There is a huge development down at the dockside where once, and only once, a shipment of slaves were housed in a warehouse that was built to store wool and cotton bales. You can guess how I know about the slaves. I have seen them. The place should be called Unfinished Business. Instead some happy marketing chappy called it Donovan's Wharf, after a misremembered John Wayne film.

We made a good living at The Glade. We had even been approached by the Donovan's Wharf development asking if we would be interested in opening up a branch down there. It was

Sam's idea to make it a franchise. They could buy the rights to have a Donovan's Glade tea room down at the wharfside and pay us a fee for doing so.

We sold the franchise to a young couple who lived in Dobbin Drive in a semi with pillars at the door. All the houses on Dobbin Drive had pillars at the door, great Ionic columns with poky-looking UPVC doors between. Dobbin Drive was a favoured location.

It was Mr Anstey who got me onto the waiting list for the allotments. Sam bought me leather gauntlets for gardening and a coffee table book on the Vegetable Year. We had no idea that the allotments would be my chance to dig a tunnel. Out of here.

May, the fifth.
And also the second

IT TOOK a year on the waiting list, but I obtained an allotment. The two people before me died just before their names came up so I jumped ahead, by a rather ironic default I thought.

The two visited me with advice about what they had planned. I decided that I would compromise and put in what they had both planned. Therefore, I erected a shed for Mrs Branch and dug in organic matter for a crop of early potatoes in honour of Mr Beech.

Mrs Branch had clearly had a premonition about me or else had plans for my future. She was so pernickety about the shed. It had to be this size and have those windows and that door and exactly the right pitch to the roof. After searching around I eventually found something she approved of. Uncannily, once it was erected on the allotted allotment, it looked like home. Even when it was empty save for my new spade and fork (gifts from

Mr Anstey and Mr Jellico) I preferred to be there. Smelling the new wood.

Over a period of about three months I filled the shed with an array of junk furniture and an antique Swedish wood-burning stove. All very domestic. Mr Jellico and Mr Anstey had high hopes of another Glade branch. Instead, I made the shed my home. It was not very gradual and not really an unconscious event. I felt safe there. Cosy. Warm. My little stove and my enamel pans.

My diet changed again, to boiled eggs and beans and soups and once I got the hang of it I ventured into small casseroles and stews, one-pot delights that I ate sitting in the shed doorway, straight from the pan. Until, that is, I was passing the charity shop and I noticed a beautiful cutlery set in the window complete with enamel cup and plate.

I was a bower bird. I slept in a steamer chair rolled up in an old bedspread that someone had once taken a lot of care to embroider. It had found its way to the charity shop and thence, via a ten pound note, into my shed.

Sam's home now seemed to him like a vacant palace. His feet echoed around the empty kitchen. The bed, apparently, was too big without me. I didn't intend to be mean but as Sam sat in my shed on a French folding garden chair painted celadon green I felt that everything he said seemed to have come from a pop song.

I don't know what I wanted him to say.

There I go again, lying. I wanted him to say goodbye, to arrive with a bag of my belongings and to leave me to it, with my view across the carrot tops and the broad beans. Instead Sam arrived with an engagement ring.

'I want you to marry me,' he said, opening the little jeweller's box. Another box. The ring, a huge chunk of cubic zirconia. I think cubic zirconia tells you all you need to know about Sam.

What did I want from him? I didn't really want diamonds or gold. I wanted something more precious. I don't know why he loved me. He felt he deserved me, that I was his because he had chosen me, not because lightning had struck. I was like a DVD player to him, a state of the art girlfriend.

But as I have said, I didn't mean to break his heart. I was living in a shed on the allotments. I think myself that the clues were there for him.

'Did you hear me? I want you to marry me.'

I was panicking then. I was so weak and feeble that I knew if something major didn't turn up in the next five minutes then I would most likely marry Sam simply for want of a way out. It was like a vast metal man-trap opening up. And then I remembered Evan. Evan Bees saved me.

'I can't marry you Sam. I'm still married to Evan.'

'He isn't coming back. I thought you would have worked that out by now.' He smiled edgily, already knowing that he was on a loser here, but his salesman instinct unwilling to give up on that last chance of a sale.

'He's declared legally dead after seven years. It's only been five.'

'I don't want to wait two more years. I don't. We should get married now.'

I could see that he was as desperate to marry me and catch me as I was not to marry him and escape. It meant exactly the same to both of us. Finally I had the answer.

'I don't want to wait two years either.' I said it flatly and he caught my meaning instantly.

Two days later he arrived with my bag of belongings. Most of which ended up in the charity shops of the town. I pared down everything I possessed to what I needed, what I loved and what would fit in the shed.

June, the sixth. The third

THE COUNCIL found out that I was living in the shed or, to quote their letter, had 'appropriated the allotment building as my primary domicile'. This was outside the bounds of the allotment agreements and I was going to be turfed out. No pun intended. I had a visit from a couple of councillors and a social worker.

'Always fancied an allotment myself,' said the moustachioed councillor, the Tory, 'but I play golf.' As if that somehow discounted having an allotment.

'My wife does our garden. And the kids won't eat vegetables anyway. Can't see the point in growing your own when you can get perfectly good stuff from the supermarket.'

And the social worker, a woman with a huge leather satchel, sat and drank tea and looked out of the window at the sweet peas. She smiled at me once or twice, a contented smile and she said absolutely nothing. The two councillors offered apologies but admitted that there was nothing they could do. Rules are rules and not made to be broken.

'We've had a lot of trouble with the travelling families over on the FastMart carpark, you might remember they were burning effigies of the mayor last month?...Well, anyway, we can't have you setting a precedent by living here.'

There was a newspaper photographer who just happened to be passing and we all posed for a jolly photo. The next day the social worker with the big satchel came back and asked if she could have tea. Atalanta, her name was. She brought home-made scones, scones which were so good I asked her for the recipe so we could serve them at The Glade. Shortly after, she gave up social working and opted to be assistant manager at The Glade.

I had to find somewhere to live. My first thought was that I would up sticks back to The Glade. It was another shed after all, and I felt at home there. However, that was going to cause more problems, not just for me but for the Giant, Brian.

He had grown a beard after My Mother's death and he looked even more like a giant with it. I saw him now and again as he went about his forestry business. He went back to Nature, because she welcomed him with open branches. In the forest, in the moonlight, he would wander naked amongst the beech and the ash.

I saw him once or twice, as I worked late at The Glade, my head drowsing over the books or waiting for a fruitcake to come out of the oven. I was always doing that, starting fruitcakes too late in the day, waiting up until the early hours for them to be cooked. Those witching-hour fruitcakes always tasted the best, though.

I would see Brian step out from his cabin. He was quite a

hairy chap, hairy in a welcoming, attractive way, not at all reminiscent of Mr Dauntsey and his wolf pelt. Brian reminded me of someone in a fairy story who is under a spell to spend their nights as a forest creature. A man fox.

I should have helped Brian I suppose, but there was nothing to be said and somehow, on the nights when I saw him heading out into the nightness I didn't feel he needed helping. For all I know it was something he did with My Mother and he was simply keeping on the tradition. Possibly he met up with her in the moonlight and they were together.

He looked at ease, if not happy exactly. Happy is overrated. It is like the giddy cousin, laughing too hard and too long. It is better to be simply at ease.

In the Land of the Giant, Brian:
forest

It's rare I venture beyond the fences now. I have my territory and I guard it. I watch the tourists and their children carefully. I allow them in and I watch over them. they are safe here. Some come with fires, trailing caravans or pitching tents. Curled up in the underbrush like the ancients.

I have an idea to save up and buy the forest from the Trust. It's my scheme for my retirement. I don't imagine they would let me stay on after otherwise. They will bring in a new forester then. They have already started sending over trainees.

Mark, who has no feeling for trees. He wears his badges and talks of management. He ought to work at the timberyard. He trips over roots. Gets himself lost walking from the information centre to the Crackett Path. There was James, who poached the fish.

They don't know anything. They walk through without looking up or around. They look at a hedgerow and they don't see the birds or the insects there.

I'm afraid to go out. Let me be honest. I am afraid that something will happen. Not just what happened to my Maddie. I don't know if I'm afraid of dying. It might mean we'd be together. But it might mean nothing. The end. Compost.

No. I'm afraid that I might meet someone else and start the process of moving on. They all say you have to move on. You have to keep going. Life goes on. But I know if I do that there is some leaving behind to be done. She is left where she is and she is further away from me still.

I am staying here. As close as I can be. My territory.

Options

MY OPTION, and Sam kept this option very open, positively wedged it open with a brick, was to head back to Sam's until I found somewhere. Sam's theory, I know, was that I simply wouldn't find anywhere. I was just too…sluggardly. Too disorganised. We would fall back into our lovely routine. He offered to store my junk, his term for it, in his garage. I think Bonfire Night was going to be his deadline. Incinerate the evidence of my freedom.

Whatever, I didn't go back to Sam's. I packed 'my junk' into some boxes which were stored at The Glade. Then Atalanta offered me room in her flat. It was the top floor of a three-storey Georgian house. There were several rows in Old Town, down by the Zion Chapel which had stood there since 1810. Atalanta did not want anything other than to help. I had helped her make a career move, she wanted to return the favour.

I loved Zion Chapel and the minister who had preached there.

He had a lot to say and I would listen. I didn't ask why he wasn't heading straight to God instead of spending two hundred years loitering in Zion Chapel. It seemed churlish. When he stood in the pulpit he seemed already to be in Heaven.

I always sat in the same pew up on the balcony. Others came and went in their chocolate brown poke bonnets or breeches with their waistcoats and pocket watches. They sat beside me, some railed at him. There was a woman and a baby. She never said anything, she simply got out a breast and fed the baby.

Every time, it stopped the preacher. The first time I expected him to rant at her, to put away her shameful nakedness in the House of God. But he didn't. He stood in the pulpit and he watched her. They are his unfinished business. His Emma. His Luke.

Atalanta was not offended when I opted to squat in the Zion Chapel preachers' rooms. They needed a body in there anyway, to scare off the vandals. The ghosts should have done that. But no one believes in ghosts. Except me of course. They've only got me to rely on.

We dropped the boxes off and we headed out for something to eat and a drink. We headed to a new American-style restaurant and bar that the Donovan's Wharf people had developed. We stuffed our faces with potato skins and dips. For the first time I sat and simply watched the chocolate-brown-clad people. There had been a factory on the site and they seemed puzzled by the new place. A holiday from their work. Something interesting to look at after all the years of dereliction. No one seemed interested in passing messages and I felt privileged, for once, to be the only person in the room who could see these people, this small window onto another world, another edge.

This was about the point that I felt that Sam didn't have a heart unless he had one that was made of wood. If you tapped on it, it sounded hollow. I wanted Hal to come along now and tell him what for. Where are these dead people when you need them? Not that Sam was fazed by that. He didn't really believe that I was a medium. He regarded it as a sort of minor league mental illness that wouldn't affect our relationship but would affect his chances of keeping me. Only someone as sensitive and caring as Sam would take on such a liability of a woman. I know that is what he thought. I knew him so well, I should have married him.

But I didn't. I kept working at The Glade. Donovan's Glade was doing well, so I had my share of that franchise and now they were building a new shopping mall on the far side of the dual carriageway at Askey's Field. They were advertising shop premises and I sold another franchise to open another Glade there. I was, at that point, the Tea Shop Queen of Town.

Sam made wedding plans. A wedding surprise he called it. The Wedding Nightmare it became. His work friends all helped him to do it, all as thoughtless and foolish as they could be.

See what a sour old cow I am? They wanted Sam to be happy. To be happy ever after, married to me and living in a lovely house in Dollyville. So they planned and they plotted and they organised. A June wedding. One of them, Beth, was a solicitor and should have known better about the legal technicalities of marrying someone else before your first spouse is declared legally dead.

Out of sight. Out of mind. Sam was certainly out of his.

I received a formal letter asking if I could attend a meeting about the new franchise being negotiated for the Askey's Field development. This was the entirely new purpose-built mall just off the dual carriageway. Where once there had been clapped-out industrial warehousing and a vast scrapyard, now there was a temple of retailing, restaurants and a multiplex cinema.

The marketing men had been extra hard at work renaming the site. It was thought that it was called Askey's Field because good old Farmer Askey had once owned it in the dim and distant past. Then an historical researcher stepped forward and told them that it was Askey's Field because that's where his hideously butchered body had been found in 1690. The marketing men had been up all night, it was clear, when the new advertising hoardings were erected declaring that this was Heron Corner Shopping Mall.

I was arguing that the new Glade should not be called Heron Glade. I wanted it to be called Askey's Glade. I felt we owed him. The arrival of the formal letter and the mention of 'discussion' and 'negotiation' gave me new hope. I was feeling quite bolshy then. My eviction from the shed, my anxiety over Sam, grief, uncertainty…I could have made a list. My world was rocking like the boats that had once docked at Donovan's Wharf, tossed on the seas, storms above, another world of unknown fish and marine life below.

I dressed for the occasion. I had one good outfit, a smart jacket and long thin skirt which gave me the semblance of a grown woman who knows what she is doing. I should have worn a clown suit, complete with giant shoes.

I arrived at the solicitor's office and she instantly asked if we could hold the meeting at County Hall as she had to see a client there at the Magistrates' Court shortly afterwards. I assumed from the buttonhole she wore that this meeting was a court appearance that had come up unexpectedly. I assumed that she was a Robin Hood style of solicitor, defending the rights of the poor and frankly defenceless. We got into a taxi and drove across town to County Hall.

I was shown into an anteroom where a smartly dressed woman greeted me with an officially polite handshake. Then we sat down and she started to take down some particulars. She checked my right name, age, address, occupation, everything except my shoe size.

All this time I did not click that this was preparation for a civil wedding ceremony. I had been married before in a cathedral, with an emphasis on the spiritual rather than the municipal. Yes, you filled out a form at some point, but mostly you declared your love from on high with trumpeting angels. So I let her fill in the forms, with her ink pen scratching at the paper.

Then they opened the door on a larger room and there was cheering, people throwing confetti, wearing hats, chucking rice, flash photography like mini lightning bolts. It was a maelstrom. A surprise party. A practical joke. In the midst of it was Sam. I tried backing up but the door to the anteroom had been shut behind us. I bumped into the door. Locked out by the angels yet again.

The way forward seemed to be to take Sam's hand. To take the posy offered like a miniature wreath, to stand and take vows and not mean them. To be manipulated and live to regret.

I did nothing. I stood frozen like a rabbit in the headlights, a rush of serotonin surging through my veins. Sam held my hand tight, kissed my cheek. I could see the registrar's mouth moving, but no sound seemed to be coming out. Her official smile. Her neat clothes. Her neat hair. She was like a new person, fresh from the packaging. As if for the next wedding she'd be disposed of and they would tear the cellophane off a new registrar.

I looked round hoping for Mr Anstey and Mr Jellico and a getaway wheelbarrow. I hoped for Brian with his giant's arms to lift me up and take me back to Goatmill, to The Glade so I could rest my head in a pat of butter, wipe over some tables, brew tea. And at last I hoped for Evan Bees.

'But she's already married…to me.' And he would look right

into my eyes before slinging me over his shoulder and taking me away.

'Do you, Annie Colville, take this man, Samuel Webster Cartwright, to be your lawful wedded husband?'

I was choking. I couldn't breathe. I could feel Sam's hand and wanted to tear free, leave my hand in his and escape with the stump. I could feel them all watching, waiting as if the room were full only of breath and anticipation. I looked at the registrar. Her official smile was becoming more official than smile.

'I can't. I'm already married.'

Before you find yourself teary-eyed at Sam's humiliation, be informed that everyone was on his side. They all commiserated with him and looked at me as if I should be burned as a witch. Cast out as a demon. Here, I had broken his heart.

'No. She's not. He's going to be declared legally dead. It's a formality.' Sam piped up. A formality. Sam was businesslike, a man closing a great deal. My heart, full of hairline cracks already, shattered. And no one noticed.

Sam's heart suffered a clean break which was soothed and healed by Beth the solicitor. In less than three months they were married. They now have four children with another on the way and Beth is a senior partner in the law firm. One of the top firms in town. They don't live in a Dollyville box house either. Somewhere between babies one and two they upped sticks and moved to a Victorian villa in Old Town on Crimea Avenue. Tree-lined, stained-glass porch and an original conservatory.

Do I look at them with jealous eyes? I did. Not now. Besides, it would not have turned out like that for me and Sam.

It was quite late one evening when Valerie came to call. I knew instantly because she had always worn a white pinny. It was a pinny so white it glowed. She might have painted it, it was so pristine. So when she showed up at The Glade, the original shed one, I was almost heartbroken to see her chocolate brown coloured pinny and her mocha shirtwaist dress.

She wasn't. She smiled. Valerie had a warm and genuine smile, she was just built that way. She ran her tea shop because she liked to see people eat her cakes. It wasn't just business, it was pleasure. Now she was here with her unfinished business.

Only Valerie knew the recipe for those rock buns. On that night, her last night on earth, Valerie gave me the secret. She stayed with me to bake the first batch, showed me how to warm the lemon, how to pinch the cinnamon, told me how to soak the sultanas in warm water to plump them up and where to buy the juiciest sultanas in the first place. It was at a stall on the market, next to the pet foods. Run by a woman called Maeve who also sold olives that hummed with garlic, were glossy with oil and speckled with green herbs.

Valerie, if you can hear me, those rock buns were never the same. But I keep trying.

July, the seventh

IT WAS the seventh year and the spell was breaking. Just like all the fairytales I had ever been told. In December, less than six months, Evan Bees was to be declared legally dead.

I made rash decisions. I sold up everything, all The Glades including the original shed, The Glade at Goatmill. I sold that to Atalanta; she would be a custodian. She would treat it right. I sold Askey's Glade at Heron Corner Shopping Mall—I sold up everything I owned except the clothes I stood up in and a toothbrush.

I opted to live at a small bed and breakfast on the edge of town. It stood amongst a row of similar bed and breakfast establishments that caught the passing trade from the main road into town. I had one room and a shower room with no window and a fan that hissed long after you turned the light off. I ate breakfast sitting in the window of the dining room looking out onto the street. Breakfast was from seven until nine and I stayed there until Mrs Harkness, the owner, pulled the tablecloth out from under my elbows at nine-thirty each morning.

I wandered. I wandered round to Heron Corner Shopping Mall and took in all the shops. I had a cafe latte at Askey's Glade. I wandered across town, passing over the footbridge that crossed the dual carriageway and I wandered amongst the charity shops and the chemist and the shoe shops. I made my way down through the park to Donovan's Wharf and I had lunch at Donovan's Glade before I headed up the hill towards Goatmill Country Park.

I wandered round and round the ancient woodland, picking out the less popular paths, avoiding the lake and the barbecue area. I walked and walked until it was almost dark and Brian would come to search me out so he could lock the gates. I would see his torch beam most nights and like a ship entirely lost at sea I would head away from it. I became the ghost of Goatmill Park.

I would walk down the grass verge of the main road back into town. The cars buzzing past on one side, fields and farm build-ings and night sky on the other. I had nowhere to go other than my room. There was a restraining order preventing me from visiting the allotments. So I found myself following in Aunt Mag's footsteps and I made my nightly circuit of the Claybank, the Robin Hood, the Freemasons Arms, the Hark to Towler.

I didn't drink. I didn't fall that far. I would order a lemonade and sit in a corner, watching the people at the pool table, the old men in the corner, the TV with the sound turned down. The lemonade was different in each place. Sugary in the Freemasons. Sour in the Robin Hood. Flat in the Towler, with a hint of washing-up liquid. Burningly fizzy in the Claybank.

One evening after being turfed out into the rain, I saw that the puddles outside the door of the Claybank were glowing and golden. I looked up to see the streetlight above and the amazing glow it cast. I thought that perhaps there had been vodka in the lemonade to make this puddle so golden. There was no streetlight. Only the lights from the Spiritualist Church across the way.

I stood for a long moment in the driving rain looking at the golden windows, the soft glisten of that brass doorknob. A woman in a chocolate brown raincoat halted outside. She opened the door, stepped into the light to shake off her umbrella before disappearing inside. It was as if the building winked at me with that door. The rain pelted harder then, the sound of it rising in volume and up a semi-tone, angry seeming. Or excited. Urging me, anyhow.

Inside it looked like a more modern version of the Zion Chapel. Long rows of seating. A balcony area, like the circle in a theatre. The damp problem had been solved years ago with a grant for improvement from the council. The wall was white now, some original heritage white from a specialist company. Other than that it was exactly the way it had always been. Even the medium sitting on a chair was looking sleepy; and then just as suddenly was standing up and asking for Jim.

I could see the chocolate brown brigade clearly. They were seated next to their relative, or as near as they could get. It was an orderly crowd and they were all tired of this Jim person not showing up. Then of course Jim nudged me.

'I'm here. What's he want?' Strange way around this, Jim was in chocolate brown butcher's apron, chocolate brown straw boater. Jim Hobbs, local butcher in about 1910. Jim Hobbs who sold catmeat for mince and put sawdust in his sausages. Not that I was aware of it at that moment. That came with research, later. Jim was asking for the medium.

'What does he want?'

I stood up and asked the question.

'What do you want?'

'You want to speak to Jim?' he seemed uneasy at the prospect.
He was in fact lying and had no message from anyone except his
bank manager. This man pretended to be a medium and made
up most of his messages trusting in the willingness of people to
spill beans and fill in gaps.

'You wanted to speak to Jim? He's here,' I said. 'Jim Hobbs,
the butcher. Is that the right Jim?'

The medium, Alan Carney was his name, was utterly silenced.
He kept looking down at me.

'I...I...' was about all he could manage.

'Has he got a message for me or what?' Jim Hobbs asked.
'Only I'm a very busy man. I've got a shop you know.'

I looked up at the medium. At Alan Carney.

'You said you had a message for Jim.'

'From Jim. My message is from Jim for someone in the
congregation.'

Jim Hobbs looked very put out at this and another chap in a
chocolate brown security guard uniform leaned down from the
balcony now and chipped in.

'I'm Jim. Perhaps the message is for me.'

'Fine. I've got another Jim now Alan. He says perhaps your
message is for him.'

Alan Carney looked ill then.

'You've got this the wrong way round,' he said. 'Can you please
sit down, this is a message *from* Jim to someone in this congregation.'

'Who? Isn't he giving you a name?'

Alan Carney's face was turning a mixture of puce and ash grey.
The congregation were moving from polite silence to restive
whispering.

'I have a name. Jim. Does anyone here know a Jim?' But the congregation were resolutely unresponsive. No one was owning up to knowing a Jim. The two Jims, the butcher and the security guard, looked at me.

'Can't you sort this? You seem to be on the right wavelength.' The security guard Jim was coming down the side stairs under the window to join us on the main floor of the church. Alan Carney was looking down from the platform at me. I was not going up onto the platform. He looked like a lemon up there. A sour and foolish lemon. I looked round at the audience. They were anxious, waiting. One or two were whispering and a few clutched their bags tighter or folded their arms, defensive or challenging.

Which is when I saw him. Up at the back in his usual seat.

He was cheery looking, handsome, hair with a slight wave to it, slicked back. He had on a chocolate brown tweed jacket and a waistcoat with a pocket watch. He was looking very relaxed and he smiled at me. He smiled as if he knew me. Which of course he did.

When I looked round a queue had formed, chocolate brown, beside me. I looked at the first woman. She was waiting, very patient. Behind her a tall man was looking at his pocket watch.

'What's your hurry?' I asked. He looked up from the watch. Suddenly I knew. It's like being in the airport. No matter how many magazines you buy and how much coffee you drink, in the end you want to get on that plane and arrive. You don't want an endless journey. But sometimes you have to say your farewells to the people at the gate. I looked at the patient woman.

'Can I deal with him first?'

Sidney sat at the back the whole time as I worked my way through the queue. As the last couple of people drew nearer Sidney joined the end of the queue. I got to him last. I was very tired now. There was hubbub in the Spiritualist Church. My messages had been specific and precise. Sidney smiled at me now and offered a hand.

'I'm Sidney Colville, Annie. Thought I'd pop back, give you a hand.'

That night, everyone got their message. Everyone.

Some of the messages they didn't want. I saw it in their faces. In the turning away, the looking down. The setting in stone of their public face. I considered then. As a messenger, perhaps I should have edited the highlights. But I thought only of myself. I didn't want to be plagued with other people's unfinished business. It isn't *my* gran shaking me awake in the middle of the night to hiss at me, 'Over my dead body.'

I pass the baton. Run with it.

I stayed all night in the Spiritualist Church. It lent itself to our talk. The staff there then, the lovely Marcia who did the caretaking, thought that you couldn't really argue with the Dead. You needed patience and other things to be getting on with. She waited up that night. The next morning she gave me my own set of keys.

Sidney Colville. The extra large medium.

He wasn't extra large. He was tall and stockily built and certainly well dressed. He had made a lot of money in his time. He had once owned North Ashton Manor complete with staff and grounds. He had been the Lord of the Manor, running two households: the one with Kitty and the one with his first wife, Edna, and their three kids. Edna and the kids had a new semi-detached in town. Edna's choice, it must be allowed. Sidney had bought North Ashton Manor House with a view to having all his family under the one roof but with rooms enough to keep them apart. Edna was having none of it, she hated the old house and wanted a new one. The minute the villas went up in Bartlett Avenue she was in there. Kitty enjoyed the Manor House.

Sidney never abandoned Edna. She was kept in a manner to which she quickly became accustomed and she had freedom. Mind you, this is his version and he was trying to impress me that first night. He wanted to be the mentor, passing on his knowledge, his expertise.

He admitted that as a kid he'd been able to see people that were invisible to others. Those people always wore chocolate brown clothing. I was interested that he too saw the Dead as I did. He said he had not had an 'open frequency'—the first time anyone had used a technical-seeming term for what I could do.

'I could shut up shop. Do they nosey in, then? Sit around and watch what you're up to?'

I had to admit then that they didn't. I was allowed some privacy. In bed with Sam. With Evan, spreadeagled on the kitchen table.

I can imagine what Mrs Berry would have said encountering me like that. 'I've just scrubbed that down. You'll get splinters.'

Or was it just that I was so embroiled in passion that I didn't see them or hear them? Maybe they were always there watching. Perhaps that was a subconscious reason to stick with Sam, he was a brief escape route. Then I remembered the sleepless nights with Hal or Aunt Mag tugging at my sleeve.

'I'd get on with it if I were you. You're never going to be settled doing anything else. You have to accept that you don't have a choice. This is a given. Some people are meant to be opera singers or concert pianists but it never bothers them because they never start to sing or they don't ever sit at a piano. They take up teaching or open a travel agency and they are none the wiser. You're always going to have to work round this.'

He had lovely eyes, my Great-uncle Sidney. They were warm

and they never let you go. He never cast sidelong glances to see if there was something more interesting than your face. I like those kind of eyes. Plus I knew he was making sense. That I had in a way been avoiding the obvious.

I wasn't a waitress or a zookeeper. I was a medium. A translator. Get on with it.

Sidney Says:
the Extra Large Medium

I haven't told her the truth. I haven't told her because I think she already knows it and won't admit it. Yet. Let her work it through at the Spiritualist Church. She's going to shock them, I think. She steps back and lets them in, whereas I was always too scared. Where would I go if they stepped in? I was nearer to the Dark Ages I suppose. The first electric-lightbulb century was just switching on. I thought I'd end up possessed. Which I was in a way, because Kitty took me over. Nowadays there's all sorts of jiggery pokery.

I always had an open frequency. I just chose to ignore it. I wandered along through life thinking it would go away. When I was fourteen there were so many soldiers. In khaki brown. I was a lad. I thought if I ignored it, laughed hard enough. Which works up to a point. If you're sitting in a room you don't listen to all the conversations.

I shunned them. I was a coward. I let them go away disappointed. But I always had bad dreams about strange people telling me all manner of rubbish.

Edna was mortified when it all came out. Not just about Kitty, that she could live with. She didn't like sex and it meant that was one less chore to be done around the house. I think it was babies that put her off. How we managed three I'll never know. I don't know what happened, something went wrong in that department for her after the first baby. I was never going to find out what because you just didn't talk about such matters. But fair play to the woman, she kept with me. She let me.

No, the sex she could do away with and she always got on all right with Kitty. Who didn't? It was the mediumship she had a struggle with. In the end the only way to make it everyday was to turn it into a parlour trick. To come up with that name, the Extra

Large Medium. I was like a fire eater or a juggler instead of a candidate for the asylum.

This girl, she's got more than I had. She's the one who can inherit my title although I'd be happier for her if she could find her Kitty, someone for her to hold onto in the Land of the Living. A lifeline.

Don't take me the wrong way though, I enjoyed it all in the end. I liked being of use. I made money. I had my family. Love and usefulness. What more could a man ask?

To let

I ARRIVED AT the Spiritualist Church late. There was a delay at the bed and breakfast with Mrs Harkness. She was growing rather tired of me but finding it hard to reconcile that with being not at all tired of my regular cheques. We had these occasional 'chats' where she dropped broad hints about my possible plans and I cruelly and heartlessly refused to give her the answers she wanted, or admit I had long ago taken the hint. It was getting more bitter as she realised that I did indeed get the message but wasn't shifting.

That day she had let my room and packed my bags. I could have really frightened her and moved my belongings into her shed. As it was I returned to the salvation of Zion Chapel. Anyway, that made me late.

'…easier if you take my tights off.' I stepped in on the end of a rudish joke.

I looked at the medium on the platform. A woman, tall and

well built, wearing an unsmart red jacket in a man-made fibre. It was a size too small and crackled with static as she moved her arms. She had a microphone, I noticed, not a device I'd seen here before. She was moving across the platform now, like a stand-up comedian.

The jokes became, well, pornographic. Bernard Manning would have blushed at a couple. I thought perhaps she'd come in the wrong building. There was a comedians' night at the pub, the Claybank across the road. She had clearly got off the bus on the wrong side of the road.

'So. I have a Joe here. Joe wants to talk. Anyone here fancy claiming Joe?' She had a gruff manner, like someone announcing a special offer over a supermarket tannoy. I couldn't see Joe. I could see quite a queue of people standing beside the platform, all in chocolate brown, and they were whispering and chatting amongst their ranks, shaking heads and looking puzzled. I was puzzled too. There was no Joe.

I had been ignorant until then. I had thought that there were people who spoke to me, and other people who spoke to other mediums. I had thought that Alan Carney's confusion over the Jims was because he simply saw different Jims. I thought there was a restriction on who came to see you. I had imagined there was an order to it.

Now I stood, and it was a revelation. There was no Joe. She didn't hear anyone. She was making it up. The rude jokes were not her misguided attempt to put everyone at ease and win them over. The rude jokes were filler. Making a little dent in the time she was going to have to stand there and try and get something out of the audience, something she could start her story with.

There was no Joe.

She didn't stop speaking into the microphone the whole time. Not even after I walked up onto the platform. I was wearing my grown-up's outfit, the jacket and the skirt. Very smart. Very sane. As I stepped up she looked a bit askance but kept on.

'…I'm sorry Joe, whoever it is you want to talk to isn't here tonight…do you have a name for me, Joe? Can you tell me who it is you want to talk to?…Eileen. Do we have an Eileen here?'

I could see a woman in the fourth row flinch slightly but she didn't own up. Obviously she was called Eileen. The Microphone Medium picked up this wavelength straight off. She pointed at Eileen.

'You are called Eileen.' Eileen nodded in terror. Which made this seem like an impressive performance. The Microphone Medium, who was in fact called Maureen, had her mark and was on a roll.

'I have Joe here…is it Joe?…I might be hearing this wrong. Sounds like Joe. Do you know a Joe? Might be someone in the family, not close…Have a think love…' While Eileen sat and shook her head with the look on her face of a schoolgirl caught out not knowing her eight-times table, Maureen made as if to talk to the imaginary Joe.

'Is that right love? You're…you're not Joe…Say again, I've got a fuzzy line tonight…no love, it was that last Guinness yesterday evening…I think it might be a Jerry. Is that right love, Jerry?'

Maureen turned back to Eileen, who looked even more puzzled and said, 'Harry.'

Like a tenpenny fortune teller Maureen read Eileen's reactions. Eileen, unconsciously, did her own reading and Maureen filled in a message, something bland and loving and coverall, something that wouldn't have looked out of place on a greeting card from the market hall. Ha, I even managed to rhyme it. Maureen shied just short of that.

But I was still standing there. Every now and again she shot me a challenging look as if she was unwilling to give up her spot.

Eventually she had to. They called for tea and biscuits. I was nervous standing up there and the queue of chocolate-brown-clad people was getting restive. Not that they were going anywhere in any great hurry. But old habits die hard. Get on with it.

So I did. Forget the tea break. As they all stood around or queued for their refreshment I just got on with it. It felt easier because they weren't all sitting there listening. Half of them weren't paying any attention. Eileen was recovering her composure with her little group of friends and others were chatting and moaning together about the narrow choice of biscuits and the lack of really juicy messages from the Great Beyond.

'Who's first?' I asked. First up was a smartly dressed old man in what looked like his de-mob suit. He had clearly had his wear out of it. He smiled.

'I want to speak to Michael. He's up at the back there blowing his nose.'

I looked up at the back there and indeed, there was a dark-haired man with a moustache blowing his nose into a cotton handkerchief.

'What do you want to say to him?'

'I want that money to go to Deirdre. The house. The lot. Just like it says in my will and if he doesn't do it I'm going to come back and haunt him and his missus.'

He said it in a matter of fact way, very polite.

'Michael,' I said. Without the benefit of the microphone. Michael couldn't quite hear me. He was laughing pompously at something that a friend was saying. I shouted.

'MICHAEL.'

There was a moment's silence. I was the intermission. They turned with their tea and their half-dunked biscuits. There were two Michaels, it seemed. A shorter, red-haired bloke looked up at me. Mouthed, 'Me?' and pointed at his chest. I shook my head and pinched a bit of business from Maureen. I pointed at my mark.

'You,' I said. 'I have a message from...'

'Dad. Harvey if he wants proof,' interjected Harvey from beside me. He was looking towards Michael.

'...your dad, Harvey.'

I repeated the message word for word, extremely specific and to the point. Harvey smiled thanks and left. Next up.

'Hannah. Your mum says to tell you that you must look in the cardboard suitcase that is in the back of the airing cupboard.'

'Mrs Willis. Sandra says put up or shut up.'

'Alison. He's a liar.'

That was quite a good one. It was personal and direct and seemed to have nothing to do with anything that anyone except Alison could know about. Alison it turned out was not even there for herself, she had simply accompanied her gran for the evening.

'Bridget, I can't believe you've chopped down that clematis when all it needed was a bit of pruning.'

I rattled along in this vein. Shed keys. Garage contents. Attic treasures and enough Crown Derby, Royal Doulton, Minton and Wedgwood to start a small antiques shop. No one came back to their seats. They all simply stood about in the raggle taggle of the tea break letting their cups get cold, their biscuits dunked to destruction, watching and waiting as message after message came through.

The queue of chocolate-brown-clad people shortened. I felt...I felt...Free. Like something bottled up finally unstoppered. A genie.

'Arthur.'

There didn't appear to be an Arthur. Still the name kept on in my head. Maureen looked very smug at this point. However, my success rate had been so huge that evening that everyone wanted to hear about Arthur's message and attempt to find an Arthur in the neighbourhood that might be *the* Arthur. But no message came. I couldn't see anyone connected to the voice I heard. I just heard 'Arthur'. Then it stopped. There was no queue. I was finished for the evening. There were smiles. There were stares. There was a snub from Maureen who got her coat and headed off very swiftly. Comment was made that she hadn't left her donation for the tea and biscuits.

Marcia sat me down. Brewed tea. Offered me her secret stash of fruitcake. Rich with lemon zest and sultanas. Slivered almonds. And we wondered, who was Arthur?

Dig Deep with Arthur:
editing the lowlifes

It isn't hard to rationalise. I think the scientific people who dismiss all this don't look at the simple facts. We don't use something like ninety percent of our brain power. Our minds have resources that simply don't show up on scans of any kind. If you want to know if God exists, look at a brain, preferably one that is functioning. You watch the fireworks, the engineering and you tell me there isn't a God. The way I see it Annie's brain is just wired up a different way. She's like a satellite dish.

I'm not afraid of this skill. It is a skill, a given. What scares me is how people have shut her off. They use her like a telephone, an object to get them what they want and then be left on a worktop, a sideboard.

What does Annie want? Don't think they'd ever ask themselves. She's learnt to be afraid of herself and has not learnt how to handle this easily. It has taken her all this time to work it through and find out how to shut down the system.

And her problem is not that she can speak to the Dead, her problem is that she cares about them all. She can't stand there reeling off the information. She wants a purpose. She wants to be useful.

Out

A FTER THAT, people came to be fed as much as to find solace. I brokered a deal with The Glade and Atalanta to supply the meetings with refreshments. I started to get a crowd. People would come specifically to my meetings. I started off on Mondays and Thursdays at first but after three months I offered my services every night of the week.

It made things easier. Somehow the chocolate brown brigade worked out that they'd get the best of the deal if they tackled me on the platform at the Spiritualist Church; that really there wasn't much point haranguing me in the street or disturbing me at the library, because I couldn't carry the messages then. Not unless they happened to be for the librarian or the caretaker or the woman on the checkout.

You have to be careful. You can't just blurt it out in the supermarket or at the cigarette kiosk. One minute they're there, packing up someone's groceries with a 'can I help you' customer service smile and the next they're hearing, from a perfect stranger, that their Uncle Neville was actually their dad. The world tilts sideways. They might fall off.

Which is why I started to use the suggestion box at the supermarket and the noticeboard at the library. I took out small ads in the local newspaper. I would just write out the message on a slip of paper, addressed to the right person and then put it in the suggestion box, pin it to the noticeboard. I always used the names and I signed it simply 'Messenger'.

Coward. Pretender. Cheat. I got my comeuppance.

A Tuesday night. I have never much cared for Tuesday. Tuesday. Night. Raining. I had been lying awake enjoying the sound the rain made as it drummed on the roof and battered down the new plastic guttering. It splattered against the window, the tempo altering slightly with the movement of the storm, thicker cloud, heavier rain, thinner cloud, it petered out, like some complicated dance or a Harrison Birtwistle symphony. He would simply have called it *Rain* and had an orchestra filled entirely with drums and triangles.

There was fierce knocking then, at the door. Someone was banging and banging and banging. I hadn't realised anyone knew I was here. I didn't think there was anyone who would want to see me. Sam had Beth now and didn't bother. My Mother was dead. Brian was the night fox, no doubt gone to earth on a night like this.

Evan Bees. My God. It is Evan Bees.

Which of course is the single most stupid thought that ever entered my head. It can only be excused by the fact that I was half asleep, warm with the sound of the drumming rain, my brain only half there. I didn't even pull on my jacket for warmth. I started out of the room, down the little creaky wooden stairs with my track suit bottoms and my T-shirt on and nothing on my feet even. I forgot to slip my feet back into my shoes. I left them, humming, under the bed.

The knocking came again and I heard a voice shout out. I shouted too, 'I'm coming. Wait. I'm coming.' Only it wasn't my voice that came out.

Preacher's. He stepped right through me on the stairwell. I felt the numbness as he stepped inside and the tingling as he hurried on out again, off down the stairs ahead of me to answer the door.

'Wait.'

My heart lurched into my mouth and started drumming in time with the rain. Then it was drumming in time with the knocking and with the tatter-tatter-tatter of Preacher's feet as they hurried down the stairs. He missed the last step, skidded a little, banged his elbow on the door jamb.

I could have stayed where I was. I could have sat myself down on the stairs right there and not bothered. I could have gone back to bed and hidden under the covers until it was all over.

I followed him out.

As I reached the edge of the balcony, the rows of wooden panelled pews, I could see him moving through the floor of the church. He had skirted down the side of the pulpit, down the twisted stair and was skimming along the edge of the main pews. There were two aisles, one left and one right, that looked up at the double pulpit, the lower level with its open Bible for the reader. The upper level, right in front of the square-paned window, for the preacher.

I moved quietly now, glad of my bare feet. I stepped down the wooden stairs and moved as silently as I could along towards the pulpit stairs. As I reached out for the handrail I was startled by the knocking again and the sound of a woman outside, angry.

I halted; Preacher reached the door. He opened it and as he pulled back so someone outside pushed in. He was nearly sent reeling.

The rain washed in and lightning illuminated two young women. Right away I recognised the woman I had seen breast-feeding the child in Zion Chapel. I saw the difference straight away. This time she did not have the child. This time she was great with child. Her round belly, rigid as a rock, was jutting out from her clothing.

She gave a cry, moved towards the back pew supported by her friend. She grabbed for the rail at the back of the seats, clung on and half stooped, working her way through her contraction. She could not speak. She did not groan. The wood groaned for her as if all her pain and noise were sent down through her white hands into the wood.

Preacher stood looking at them both, not even shutting the door. The rain was soaking the back of his clothes as he stood there. The woman's friend turned and yelled at him.

'Shut the door. You'll not turn her out now.'

The door shut. The woman giving birth leaned against the pew, breathing hard.

'Again,' was all she said before bending, squirming, trying to find a place to stand that would ease the birth pains. There was a Mexican standoff going on between Preacher and the friend. Finally the woman giving birth simply let herself slide to the floor. The baby was coming out and there was nothing they could do.

Her friend was at her side now, pulling back her clothing to see what was happening, what needs must be done. Preacher tried to move away but Friend stopped him.

'Nothing you haven't seen before, Preacher.'

He stopped then, and she turned away. 'All right Emma, all right now then...'

I watched from the pulpit. There was hardly a noise. The drumming of the rain and the whispers of the friend as she tried to help. Emma did not yell or groan. Instead she made odd, tight sounds like a strong man in a circus lifting a weight. You could hear every sinew of her body pushing at the baby.

Still, it wouldn't come out. Friend's whispers faded out. Instead she kept silent, her hand keeping contact with that bouldered belly, her face downturned, all her energies concentrated on the birth. There were odd slick noises, blood, shit. Friend was reaching in now, feeling for the baby. Her hands coming back out bloodied.

Then silence.

It was an hour-long minute afterwards. I thought it was the rain I could hear, still pattering. But it was Friend's tears on the wooden floor. Friend crying. A thin gasping, her face downturned to Emma. She reached, pulled Emma's skirts back over her belly.

Not once did she look at Preacher.

Not once did Preacher take his eyes from Emma's body.

I think it was the next day that Sam came to tell me that he and Beth were having a baby. After my historical night I reacted badly. Sam took this quite well, assuming that my white-faced muttered congratulations were signal enough that I was jealous.

I was thinking that it is easy to be happy if you can obliterate everything that is going on around you. As Sam stood there, he was not grieving for Emma and her baby. He wasn't thinking that maybe this year was a tough year for me, that this year they would declare my long-lost husband legally dead. No, Sam thought about Sam and Beth and their closed-in universe. How all the planets were in orbit around Sam. And I was a black hole sucking in everything and never being filled up.

*

I was still at the Spiritualist Church then. Still doing my party piece and reuniting lost soup tureens with their rightful inheritors. But I don't know, the Emma incident with Preacher had opened something up. Something even more like a black hole, I think. People started to arrive that I couldn't control. They wouldn't wait in line for each to take their turn. I had to struggle along, pushing my way past them to get to the ordinary people.

'GO AND GET HER.'

'FIND HER. FIND HER.'

'Listen to me. Are you listening? Listen to me.'

'Why can't you go there? Why can't you?'

People who didn't have Crown Derby or shed keys. People who didn't seem able to string more than one sentence together. They all arrived with their separate, incoherent mantras.

How can I get her if I don't know who 'her' is?

The platform at the Spiritualist Church was not the place for this. The congregation did not want to sit and listen to me try and figure out the verbal puzzles.

'Snakes and Ladders. It is. Snakes and Ladders.'

'Aubergine. Aubergine. Aubergine. Aubergine. Aubergine.'

It reached a stage where I stood on the platform and I separated them out. The congregation looked on as I simply said, 'All family matters this side. You, you, you and you…wait this side. I will deal with you later.'

After the congregation had left I would sit down in the front seats and I would have them all come to me. I would try to sort things through with them: I need a name; I need information.

What I got was mysteries and puzzles. Sometimes it simply helped them to talk as if I knew what was going on.

'Listen to me. Are you listening?…'

'Yes. What is it?'

'Listen.'

And that would be that. Except it wasn't. For one evening I asked a question and it was only later that I found out the answer. The horrible truth. In the horrible truth I found my future. My reason. The way forward.

'Who is she? Tell me who she is and I will find her for you,' I said one night to a distraught lady in her late fifties. She had come on a couple of nights now and was distracted, winding her wedding ring round and round on her finger. The first two nights she came she had gone before I got through the family matters and the never-ending hunt for Jims. We had five Jims that night.

'Can't. Don't know who she is. Find her. Find her.'

'Do you know where I should look?'

She was crying now, very distressed, couldn't speak for several moments, dried her eyes with the back of her hand.

'He goes fishing.'

At which she broke down completely and sobbed.

'Where does he go fishing?'

She got up then and, struggling to breathe through her emotion, was gone.

Did I say she was gone? I lied.

Next night. Congregation half asleep. Evening drawing to an end. Tea urn on. Marcia putting out cups. I was in the middle of a tedious domestic drama about a hedge which was going to be an eternal unfinished business since the dead husband and the living wife were never going to agree about it.

'Chop the bugger down,' someone shouted from the back and a laugh went up. I felt suddenly weary. I needed to sit down. I don't know what it was, a lapse in my concentration or what, but the next moment I was utterly numb and she was speaking through my mouth. She had a deeper voice, anxious sounding.

'Find her. Find her. Don't know who she is. Find her. Find

her. HE GOES FISHING.' And she was gone again.

This time I was left on the floor, such was the energy she zapped into and out of me. I wondered if that is what it feels like to survive a lightning bolt.

The church was in uproar. Several people were crying and shouting. Marcia had knocked over a dishwasher basket of clean cups and they were smashed everywhere. I did not realise, but nothing like that had happened here before. In the past it had always been so civilised with the Dead meekly queueing and the living enjoying their tea and biscuits. Not once had they had a genuine voice from beyond. 'Scared shitless' is the phrase that best describes them. Mass exodus.

Only Marcia was sanguine, heading into the kitchen for the dustpan and brush. She was left to revive me, propping me up on her knee, offering her own personal mug brimful of hot tea with no sugar, just the way I liked it. We sat there for a good while, me resting against her, Marcia squatting down, legs bent under her stroking my hair.

'There you go,' she said. 'Feeling better?'

I wasn't really. I was feeling curious. Anxious. I felt this was an important message and I wasn't getting it right. I wondered if it was to do with Evan Bees, if maybe I was the one I had to find to tell me that he was going fishing and could be found sitting under a vast umbrella on a riverbank.

I dreamt that night that I found him under that umbrella on that riverbank, only when he opened his mouth to speak it was full of bait. Worms writhing, before I woke up with a start. Then of course I imagined that was the message. He had been drowned whilst fishing. Fished out of the water. Eaten by a fish. Eaten by worms.

It worsened. For two days at the end of that week I ate nothing but Bourbon biscuits.

Then I happened to be driving past Goatmill. I hadn't been there for a long time. I occasionally popped up there to have tea at The Glade and say hello to Atalanta, but I had stopped doing it quite so frequently. The nostalgia depressed me. It seemed to me then that I looked back on bad times and forward to nothing.

But as I drove past that afternoon I suddenly noticed the fishing sign. I had forgotten that the lake was fished. I had forgotten the men with their baskets and shelters and their coolboxes full of mealworms. The memory of it broke my dream. After the intensity of the past few days I felt that a walk around the lake would be a good idea. If it didn't answer my question then it would at least make me feel wakened. It would clear out my thoughts if I didn't find Evan there.

I might have guessed who I would find there if I had been in possession of a television. People denigrate television but in fact it is an informative little box. It informs you of all the doom and disaster from a local to a global level. If someone has died in a house fire round the corner from you, or if a thousand starving refugees have crossed a distant border, you can guarantee that television will bring you full-colour moving pictures.

Moving in the sense of not being static. Moving in the sense that in the wave of guilt and depression that sweeps over you at the misfortune of others you move your thumb and move to another channel. A channel where you can see earthquake victims being deluged by a gigantic mud-slide.

There was a dog barking. Barking and barking at nothing. His master, an older man with a pipe and a tweed hat, was talking quietly to the dog, trying to calm him and also puzzled at what was getting to him. The dog was barking at the lake, rushing to the edge and barking but not wanting to go into the water.

Bark. Bark. Bark. Other fishermen, dotted around the edges of the lake were getting bored of the noise. Bark. Bark. Bark.

When I saw her, I wanted to bark too. There was no way I could speak to her, not with the dog and the Fisherman sitting there, so I simply parked myself on a tree stump at the edge of the trees and waited. It was going to be near dark before they left. As he stood up, stretched and started to pack away his things the dog became a little more frantic. He had to drag it away, off down the path towards the carpark.

I stepped forward. She was just sitting at the water's edge. She wasn't wearing any clothing. There was nothing except for a clumsy necklace of bruises. She looked like a sepia photograph and she was disorientated, looked blankly at me, blankly at the water. In shock. Unable to communicate. I tried to talk to her but she simply looked at me. Shivered.

'What's your name? Can you remember?'

She shivered again, looked across the water to a patch of trees that screened the carpark. She pointed that way. Shivered once more.

'How did you get here? Do you remember?'

Which was a question I should have kept to myself for she stopped looking blank then, and a memory flickered across her face. She took in a deep gasping breath, a shocked, disbelieving breath and her face folded into tears. She slid into the lake.

He goes fishing.

In the twilight now the fishermen had packed up, or were in the process of packing up. Folding umbrellas and nifty chairs into unfathomably small parcels. Clicking plastic lids on endless boxes of worms and gadgetry. They moved like fish through the encroaching dusk, green-skinned in their khaki pants and their waxed coats, some green, some brown.

He goes fishing. And at last I knew.

I made the telephone call from the next town. I had to be careful because they are in the process of installing CCTV so that your every move can be watched, whether you are a copulating couple in a bus shelter or a drug dealer at the bandstand. I was not going to be traced. I didn't have any way to explain what I knew.

They would be scornful if anyone had listened as to how I knew. Talking to the Dead? Ha. Yeah. Right. Cross your palm with silver.

If I had been in possession of a TV I would have known that the missing girl had been on 'CrimeWatch' only the last week. I would have known that there was a special number to call. As it was I simply went to the library the next day and looked up the number of the local police station. Armed with my post-it note I walked to the next town. It isn't any great feat. About three miles up the dual carriageway.

I enjoyed the walk, it was a cool evening. I liked to leave the car behind. I didn't want the car to be seen. To be traced. Not cowardice. Just practicality.

I stood in the box and almost chickened out. The telephone seemed to ring out forever. My heart was pounding and pounding. Then finally someone answered, only I could barely hear them for the thrumming of my blood pressure in my ear. They spoke again, more carefully this time.

'I don't know her name. She is in the lake at Goatmill Country Park. He goes fishing.'

'Say again?' There were some muffled noises in the background. People scrabbling to pick up other phones. Scrap paper being found to write upon.

'The missing girl. I don't know her name. She is in the lake at Goatmill Country Park. He goes fishing.'

I spoke carefully and deliberately so that they could take down the details, enunciated clearly so that if it was taped and they played it back they would be able to hear me clearly. Then I put the phone down and walked away.

In the Land of the Giant, Brian:
forest

They broke my boundaries today. After I have so carefully guarded my perimeters, set my fences. I find that it is all useless. Today the police came. They descended just like the fishermen, clicking open plastic boxes, reeling out lines, casting nets. They had divers, faceless in scuba masks, rubber skinned. Frogmen. Does anyone still call them that?

I had not known, and now wish I didn't know, what it means to 'drag' a lake. They have a line tagged with hooks that trawl in the deep water until they snag on an object. An old boot. A rusting bicycle. A mermaid.

You half expect them to haul her out, feet first, like some hunted-down shark.

Weigh her. Measure her. Take photographs. By now the frogmen have slipped their skin and other men in white suits, crackling plastic skins anxious to be shed, take over.

We have been asked for our records for all fishing permits, the angling club. I look at the cards in the index, all neatly filled in. It is hard to imagine that one of these people is this. Has done this.

There is almost nothing we know about each other is there?

Father figures

I DREAMT NIGHTLY that I was at the bottom of Goatmill Lake. I dreamt nightly that no one was looking for me. As you can see I was heading straight for Bourbon biscuit territory with a first-class ticket.

They struggled to find the Fisherman, as he became known. The policeman at the centre of the case was Detective Inspector Knight and he was tireless and tired looking. It seemed to me that his photograph or television image was always at the periphery of my vision. He haunted me. I knew, right at the back of my heart, that I could take the furrow out of his brow. But I didn't. I was scared.

Brian was involved as they dredged through all the records of anyone who had ever fished at Goatmill—coarse, game, a stick and some string. They combed through the undergrowth with rakes and tweezers.

The town filled with investigative journalists all thinking that they could solve the insoluble and then write some stonking bestseller book, the kind that strains your back just looking at it on the shelf. They were vermin in the end, swarming over the town, picking over the rubbish.

Worst of all was the way that, unable to find the true culprit, they started to make the victim less victim-like. She was a slapper. She was a druggie. They made it up. I didn't read the newspapers. I didn't watch the television. But the information filtered through.

And then her mother came to a meeting. She sat at the very back in the seat nearest the door. She arrived after everyone else had settled down so that there was no staring or pointing.

She sat, said nothing, spoke to no one. When the tea break came she slipped out of the door before everyone got up and saw her. There was nothing for her, her daughter did not show. Marcia told me that the girl's mother came only to my meetings.

The father's hair turned white. It wasn't just the trauma. It was the fact that dyeing his hair dark brown suddenly seemed unimportant. A tide of white hair began to wash down his head, starting at the roots like a polar ice cap, and as the days got colder and his daughter was further away so the ice spread, his hair whitening and whitening until one morning he was spotted in the barber's and the last of the dark brown dyed hair had been shorn. He looked older. Wiser.

I was sitting at The Glade with Atalanta who was giving out tea and advice that I wasn't really listening to. Atalanta means very well. She has a good heart and all that, salt of the earth, but she hasn't lost anyone. She hasn't been married, except for six months shortly after she left university, and that ended amicably. She still goes occasionally on Peruvian hiking holidays with her ex-husband, Jasper. As I once pointed out to her rather sourly, at least her husband didn't go off on a Peruvian hiking holiday as a slight detour home. I thought of Evan then, in Peru. Or possibly Brazil with the last of Hitler's escapees, ancient villains kept alive with the blood of Peruvian monkeys. Or tapirs.

I'm rambling. I was rambling then. Atalanta had to serve a couple of customers then and as she was at the counter one of the journalists entered. He started to ask questions of a group of teenagers. Questions about sex sessions in the woods at night. Raves. They were questions that had nothing to do with Goatmill Park or with the girl or even the Fisherman. Unless you thought of them as bait.

The teenagers all looked puzzled, one lad laughed uncomfortably. He was pounced on. The journalist pulled up a chair next to the lad, and all his questions were aimed at him.

'Did you know her?' 'Were you her boyfriend?' 'What were you doing on the day she died?' 'You weren't fishing?' 'You got any hobbies then?' 'You go fishing at all?' 'Did you kill her?'

As he talked, his questions took on an odd sheen of truth. It is amazing how the truth is something that simply has to be spoken out loud. If he sat there for long enough and said it loud enough. All the mates around the table clammed up and the journalist sat for five uneasy minutes at their table until Atalanta approached and asked, 'Anything else?' and she wasn't talking about the menu.

I knew I had to kick into gear. I had to find that woman again and ask her. And I stopped myself there; that was not the way. I knew the way. There was a huge sign pointing out the way and I was blanking it.

It became a tug of war in my head. And then the mother waited for me in the lobby afterwards one night and we lurched over the line together.

'Please.' The word was little more than a hoarse breath. She wasn't crying now. She had drained all her tears, she was quivering and insubstantial under her surface. Waiting. Make no mistake, she knew where she was going and I was going to be the one to escort her.

'Please.'

I had known there was only one way. Go straight to the victim. I had not seen her since that day at the lake. I had not gone back to the lake because I was cowardly, afraid. In the chilly lobby as the girl's mother stood before me I was ashamed. There was only me to help them. And I was angry. Chiefly at myself.

Say something. Say anything. I had always pleaded for information. Please.

The lake was black and there was a scent of old leaves to the water, metallic and cold. The pebbly shoreline quickly gave way to big boulders and jutting rocks, hidden and bearded with weed and plants. I started off walking the perimeter, back to where I had seen her.

I stayed there a long time. Fishing season was over and since the murder no one had wanted to paddle in there. There were no rowing boats out either that day. They were tied up at the jetty by the boathouse. No one had wanted to row out onto the lake, even though her body was long gone now.

There were others in there, a couple of schoolkids had drowned in the fifties and one teenage boy on a hot day in 1976. I didn't see them. They didn't have any unfinished business. They had gone to an endless summer day where they would never have to come out of the cooling water and get dry.

The afternoon shadows shifted and lengthened. I took a rowing boat. Pushed out. Onto the lake. Across the black and glass-cool water. The oars didn't seem to make much noise as they slapped and dragged the water. The sound was oddly muffled. I rowed until my arms ached. Then I pulled the oars inside and I sat in the boat.

The girl was not shivering. She looked silvery like a fish and her eyes were as glassy black as the lake, as if she was a vessel, filled to the brim with the water. I could see from the corner of my eye that an older man walking his dog had spotted the boat. He was standing on a banking, his hand shielding his eyes from the evening sun, watching me. His dog was running onwards, backwards. Barking. Barking.

I was waiting for her to speak. Then I thought, I have spent my whole life waiting for the others to speak.

'I can help you if you tell me. I tried to find the Fisherman's wife but she's gone too. Did he kill her?'

'Did he kill me? Is that it? Is that what's wrong?'

She gave a quick shudder then, like a swimmer after a dip. She looked at her hands, the skin pruned with moisture. I hesitated to answer. It was hard enough for her to be confused, it would be harder still for her to suddenly find out she was dead.

'Is this Heaven? Looks just like Goatmill doesn't it? Are you an angel?'

'This is Goatmill. I'm not an angel but I can help you. Who brought you here? What happened? If you give me information I can help you. That's all I want. I want to do something. I want to be useful.'

She took a long moment, looking into the water, looking up at me. The lake water brimmed over in her eyes.

'What's the last thing you remember?'

'I remember you.'

It was late when I arrived at the police station and it was even later by the time I had decided I couldn't go in. Later when I picked up the phone book. Later even when I headed back out. Later still as I reached the edges of Old Park and turned into Bartlett Avenue. Detective Inspector Knight lives in Bartlett

Avenue. Two doors from where my Great-aunt Edna lived, with and without Sidney.

There was nothing for it but to ring the bell and it ringed and dinged horribly in the quiet of the night. At that time of the morning even the hum from the dual carriageway and the motorway sliproad was silent. A low light winked in a window above as a blind twitched back. I was looking up at that when DI Knight opened the door. He looked disappointed. Then showed me in.

It was a relief not to have to explain myself. He was aware of who I was and he didn't mess about. We moved through the hall to the kitchen and he began to make tea. His wife hovered, drowsy in the doorway, checking that everything was fine and then she yawned her way back to bed.

Perhaps it was pyjamas that made this easier, or perhaps it was the unreality of night. Or possibly the fact that I didn't think he'd believe me and therefore I was telling some sort of hideous bedtime story, something to give him nightmares when he returned to bed. Something to get me off the hook.

In a serious and factual way I told DI Knight that I had had contact with the Goatmill Girl and I gave him all the bits and pieces she remembered. He, in a serious and factual way, listened.

Afterwards, there was a silence. It stretched itself out like a lazy cat. I felt dizzy now, and a butterfly battered against the walls of my stomach trying to get out. What I read from DI Knight's face was that he was thinking. Not dismissing. Thinking.

'Let's face it. I have to listen to you,' he sighed at last, his shoulders bending inwards slightly under the T-shirt he was wearing. 'I'm fucking desperate.'

I had to go to the station. DI Knight wanted me to look over some of the evidence they found to see if it tallied with anything the girl had said.

Alex. Her name is Alex. Will always be.

I knew the killer was a widower because his wife started this at the meeting. Alex had offered facial details, a particular and pungent brand of aftershave that she remembered. Her left hand catching on the floor panel where the spare tyre was kept as he shoved her inside, into the darkness of the car boot. And a particular fishing box she was shoved up against for that last journey. A leather tog on his shoe.

DI Knight talked everything through with me and expected the details to be mine. He wasn't giving me anything, he wanted to be sure of what I had to give him. What convinced him was the leather tog. This was something not released to the public domain. When he heard about the tog he knew. When I saw it in a small evidence bag it jarred my nerves. It was found in the undergrowth near the edge of the lake and never discounted. The togs on the shoes. The last thing she looked at.

In order to keep credibility he began with the car. He could say, quite truthfully, that someone saw the car at the lake and had recently reported it to the hotline. I was going to be kept in the shadows, because let's face it the Crown Prosecution Service might not accept evidence from the dead victim, however true and nothing but the truth. I wanted to be in the shadows. This was not about me.

They found the car. The owner fitted the physical description I had and also, more crucially, he had lost his wife recently. However, nothing in the car seemed to be of use. Nothing seemed to be evidence. It was a neat, well-valeted car. He was a man with a power hose and a wet-and-dry vacuum cleaner. He did not have a pair of shoes with elaborate and fancy leather togs. He was not a man with an unusual fishing box. All his tackle was run of the mill. As DI Knight put it, 'Any bugger can get hold of that stuff.'

More worryingly, as the investigation began to crank up, Alex's mother came back to me. She didn't attend the meeting. She waited outside for me, waited till everyone had gone and I was alone. The first time, she leapt out on me from behind the door to the toilets. She had a febrile, desperate look.

'I want to talk to her. Let me talk to her.'

I tried to explain that it doesn't work like that. I couldn't conjure Alex out of the air. But that was not what she wanted to hear. She pinched her lips together. Left.

After the next session, and the next, she pounced on me. 'I want to talk to her.' Clipped, decisive. Trying to make me think I had no choice. I noticed that her eyes had that black, glassy look as if she too was filled with the lake water. 'I want to talk to her.' And once again I tried to explain. She was angry then, a hand whipping out to snatch at me. She was hurting my arm.

'You can't do this to me.'

Alex's father arrived at The Glade the next morning. It was clear it was quite an ordeal for him to enter Goatmill. His pleas were an ordeal for everyone else.

'She just wants to talk to her. To say goodbye, you must be able to understand that. Please. It's just relaying a message. Isn't it? Isn't it that easy? For you?'

And I didn't know what to do. Where does it end if I begin it?

DI Knight had the car stripped out, carpeting, seats, the lot. No shoe tog. But wedged into the crack between carpeting and spare wheel they found a broken-off piece of fingernail. As they commenced the DNA testing on the nail a uniformed constable found a battered old vacuum that the Fisherman's wife had used. Inside the bag, amongst the cat hairs and the belly-button fluff, was a fancy leather shoe tog.

Her mother ambushed me again. This time waiting for me outside the supermarket. I looked at her and I saw how grief was eating her alive. I knew then that I couldn't take her to the lake, that if I did, there would never be a goodbye for her. She was clawing at my clothes, repeating over and over, 'Please, please.' Her husband came towards us, tried to unpeel her from me. She was wailing, keening, a high-pitched animal sound and it was if something switched inside me.

I saw, for just a moment, My Mother. Not, I hasten to add, in any chocolate brown outfit. She was sitting at the scratched and scrubbed table in our old kitchen. Her eyes looking over the top of her reading glasses to squint at the instructions for a torch. It was a huge security light with a candlepower equivalent to that of a small lighthouse. She had ordered it specially from a mail order firm. Behind her on the stove a pressure cooker was coming up to steam, hissing and fussing. Her glasses were perched halfway down her nose and she was trying to shoehorn the batteries into the compartment. I could see her fingers fiddling.

The batteries click. She gives a triumphant grunt. Clearer than I have ever remembered her face, I see her thumb, the ridges striping the nail, the healing cut from where she sliced it open the previous week, being careless with a corned beef tin. The thumb pushes the switch, the torch light beams on. 'TA-DA,' she says, adopting a magician's-assistant pose, just as the pressure cooker explodes behind her.

Now, when I need it, when I can understand, I get the message. She does not have to come back to tell me, it is already there for me to find. That there comes a time when it is goodbye. And if you're going, go.

And it's gone.

*

The journalist at The Glade wrote his book. His angle was the mystery police informant who became known as Phone Box simply because that is the best the journalist could come up with in light of DI Knight's determination to keep quiet. All he ever said was, 'How the fuck should I know? All I know is the bugger called from a box.'

Phone Box. I ask you. If he could only know the truth, it was me, the Freakshow Kid, the Midwich Colville. If I felt the tug of the Bourbon biscuit packets, I would lift myself with the secret knowledge of what the journalist could have made out of my life. If he had just sidestepped a couple of tables and asked me a question. Who knows what voice might have blurted out through my mouth?

I liked the fact that they didn't know me, that they made things up; it tied me to her. She was not alone.

Alex's father broke down in court the day they sentenced the Fisherman. He was so overcome he had to be stretchered out, the silver gurney knocking into a couple of photographers' legs as they rushed forward wanting to be the first to capture the grief. Her mother shielded him, holding his hand. The beginning and the end for them.

I thought about if I died. There was no one going to be stretchered out on a trolley for me.

I thought about My Father.

Dig Deep with Arthur:
historical footnote

I was digging at a Roman fort in Northumbria. We were just off Hadrian's Wall. At least when I started the dig they had thought it was a fort; some beggared outpost of the empire which might have served as a Claudian or Vespasian Checkpoint Charlie. Merchants and goods in.

We kept on digging and as we brushed away more dirt we travelled farther in time and the fort expanded to a brothel and a granary and before we knew it we were brushing our way past fountainheads and courtyards on the main street of a full-blown Roman town.

I've dug a lot in my time, through choice. I've dug holes in the road, foundations for award-winning public buildings, trenches for cabling and gas pipes. Archaeology was a slight detour I'd taken that year, something almost new. After all it was still digging.

They were the best holes, though. They led somewhere. An undercover world. I liked peeling back the crust. I got a hell of a kick from it. Every bucket of dirt revealed a little bit more of the past and led me a step nearer to my future.

I liked the organic stuff best. Don't get me wrong, I loved the stonework, the bath house and the latrines. But I liked a worn-down step. I liked the sole of a shoe, a curse written on a lead tablet, a fragment of drinking glass, an amber bead, a ring. I liked the sewing needles and the broken bone combs. The everyday. The personal. The Stuff.

We all stayed at a nearby youth hostel. Cheap and cheerful ex-land army barracks with no telly. Suited me fine, although some went stir crazy without their fix of 'Newsnight' or soap opera. Me, I was happy to sit with a smoke and some cards and hear the true life soap operas from the lips of those around me.

There was Bridget Flinch. Professor of Roman Sandals. Slight woman. Small flat breasts like pockets, the nipples hard little knobbly buttons that would have your eye out, cut your lips if you dared to kiss them. Long, frazzled hair in a variety of faked browns, always escaping from its elastic-band bondage.

You watched her of a morning in the kitchen; well, I did. I would watch her flip that hair in her fingers like a snake, twisting and strangling it into a Gordian knot. I wondered why she bothered. Have it shorn off. Give yourself five more minutes for another cup of tea. A bit more toast and marmalade. She kept that hair because it was her strength. If she'd cut it she'd have vanished.

We all rubbed along, playing poker for Smarties, because no one had any cash. Cribbage. Whist. Headed a bit upmarket towards bridge. Along the way I got to know that geophysicist Andy was more in love with his sister than his wife.

You have to understand Andy didn't say this outright. No one ever does. What you say is in the pauses, the unconscious stuff, the things you don't say. Take Andy and his sister. For the first week we were there Andy and the others thought Maria was his wife. I listened harder. Maria says this, he would say. Then later, my wife doesn't do that. The two phrases never met. Never my wife, Maria. Maria, my wife. You get me? His wife is called Gwen.

Bridget doesn't have to say anything at all. She wears skin-tight tops, licks her fingers and ritually bumps her target with her backside. Andy was in the midst of the hunting ritual and didn't even know it. I'm taking mental notes. It isn't voyeurism. This is anthropology.

As the fort expanded and the trenches got deeper and longer and bigger they needed more labour. They'd put out an advert for paid volunteers, students, retired people, people with, frankly, nothing better to do.

It was a Thursday. Andy, Bridget and a group of the others

headed off to the pictures. Beer, film, curry. I was tired so I opted out, took a shower and then sat with my cards and a smoke. That I never got around to smoking.

I was going through all the patience games. I don't know anyone who really plays patience anymore, not with cards. It's all on computer, Freecell and Solitaire where the king is always twitching at you. Me, I like the cards. Cards have come with us through the centuries. Portable.

As always I ended up playing klondike. Which most people think is patience itself. Your basic seven-card stacks, red on black, black on red. You know it. I'd played a couple of abortive hands. I'm not usually prone to cheating. Seems pointless. Cheating yourself. I'm a shuffle-and-deal man.

I kept playing. Heart on a spade. Club on a diamond. Diamond on a club. Whittling down the pack. And suddenly he's there at my shoulder as if he's sprung out of the wipe-clean carpeting.

He's tall and underfed. He looks like a refugee. The dirt is ingrained deep into his clothing and his skin so you can't tell where the fabric ends and he begins. He has, in fact, a patina. He is worn and weathered. His hand offers a white piece of paper. It's Bridget's flyer about the volunteer work.

'Am I too late?' he asks me. His voice is quiet, hopeless. He sounds as if he believes he is too late. For everything.

I don't know it yet, but this is Evan Bees.

Cold calls

ONCE AGAIN I was stymied by my lack of personal relics. I didn't have a neat, beribboned parcel of love letters from Dad to My Mother. I had the various fairy stories she had told me. I began there trawling the directories and lists of universities looking for Professor Dad.

I had no hint at his name. On a personal level I could remember Mr Bentley and vile Mr Dauntsey and our lovely Giant, Brian. All could be struck from my list straight away. I quickly realised not just how much of my own life had been hidden from me but how much of My Mother's life was missing. Spaces. Gaps. Blanks. I began to feel like a character in a time-travel film who discovers they are fading the more they become entangled in the past. The past is where we should not be.

I had a taxing time that month. My mind was so occupied with the hunt for Dad that the Dead got a foothold. I folded into bed each night and yet I couldn't unfold in the morning.

The night was missing to me. I couldn't quite remember what had been said, who had visited, exhausted me, worn me out. I didn't care then. I let them come and let them have their say. I can recall odd faces in dreams.

I have dreams now. Instead of customer service sessions full of people shouting at me, making complaints about things that I have no power over.

I made a list of all My Mother's lame ducks and cold-called them to try and prise clues from them.

I find the telephone a strange instrument. I know you will laugh considering that my chief source of conversation is with dead strangers. No, a telephone brings the person close enough to whisper in your ear. A telephone call invades your space. The voice is in your head.

It felt strange to hear Chris Baker's voice after so long. And of course, now that I'm grown up I could hear the wary tone in her voice. Her unwillingness to remember me, the Freakshow Kid. For just a second I could hear her deciding whether or not to remember My Mother. She is not remarried but she is 'settled'. I think her use of the word 'settled' was a subtle hint to me to keep quiet and not pass on any messages I might have received. Do not unsettle me, Freakshow Kid.

She gave me two names, Paul Whelan and Alan Hartley. Chris had known My Mother before I was born. These two seemed likely candidates; and also a mystery man in a Rover 2000 who she thought might have been called Howard. I noted it down even though she couldn't make her mind up if that had been his first or surname. Then Chris Baker was very anxious to be gone and may possibly have moved house so that I can't ever call her again.

I took longer to find Janey Kirkpatrick. In the end I saw a photo in the paper of a teacher at Sir Charles Whitworth High with his prize-winning science class. *Mr Kirkpatrick with his students and their National Award.* They were all standing there like ill-at-ease prats in one of those idiotic stances that local newspaper photographers are specially trained to obtain. Hold your certificate up higher. Grin. Move closer together because there isn't much room in the paper for this sort of thing between the adverts for double glazing and garden fencing.

Mr Kirkpatrick and his prize-winning class were blowing up a chemistry lab when I arrived. It was odd to think back and remember him as a red-haired chess team teenager. His brother lives in Germany now and his sister lives in a commune in Devon. Obviously a hangover from their time in the spare rooms of My Mother's house.

Mr Kirkpatrick was helpful. He was helpful because he had a lady friend who was doing some sort of brain research at the university. He wanted me to be an experiment, let her measure my brainwaves when the Dead were speaking. I agreed. He telephoned her first and arranged our meeting before he gave me his mother's telephone number.

Janey Kirkpatrick lives at the coast now and throws pots.

I took the train to the coast. It is about an hour with the train halting at every stop just so you can stare at the benches and marvel at the wonders in other people's back gardens. I have not travelled much, but I like the train for its sneaky back view.

She sobbed when I introduced myself, 'I'm Annie Colville. Madeleine's daughter.'

Janey had a studio on the ground floor of a three-storey fisherman's cottage. It was in the harbour in Old Town. It was like a fairytale cottage, as if at any given minute a talking fish would be begging a boon of thee. She made tea, poured from a pot she made herself into mugs she made herself.

Apparently it was all due to My Mother that Janey was happy

here, now, doing this. My Mother's encouragement and support. Here I was being shown two things I didn't ever know about My Mother.

Janey Kirkpatrick upset me further when she got out an album of photos and picked through them. There were photos of My Mother with Janey's kids. One or two at Goatmill before it was officially a country park. Others showed her at events, a car boot sale manning a stall, a jubilee of some sort with flags and children in costumes. I looked for myself amidst the fairies and the monkeys. Am I standing behind Batman? At the side of the boy dressed as a snooker table?

I remembered the festival. We were all in a steamy beer tent hiding from the rain. Outside mud slathered. What did I wear that day? Where am I in the photo? I am not there. I am missing.

She had one of the two of us. My Mother crouching in the garden weeding out one of her barrels. She looks happy and relaxed. It captured her so perfectly, the way her hand is raised, the half smile, that I gasped. I wanted to cry. I am standing a short way behind her looking serious. What I saw is that I looked like a ghost. A little haunting girl, hanging around in the background spaces.

Janey went to night school to learn the art of ceramics and pottery. She took it up as a hobby on the advice of My Mother and found she had talent. I remembered the evenings we spent playing cards or Monopoly with Janey's kids. They must have been Janey's pottery nights. And in return Janey babysat when My Mother dated a handsome 'old friend of the family'. Oliver Howard and his Rover 2000.

So, we have a name that has cropped up twice and been lent history. Janey told me he had known My Mother since she was a girl. My brain mistranslated 'girl' into that stage of girlhood when you are in fact a young woman. When you are sixteen and your body has all the shape and function, but your brain doesn't emotionally match up to it. Your brain can still get a kick out of riding the playground roundabout until you are dizzy, as men are dizzied by your hips.

Again I was at the edges of territory that I had never seen before, My Mother as a Girl. I began to feel that I was looking through the wrong end of a telescope and that my life was further away.

It was pushed still further by Miss Chatham, now Head Librarian and County Archivist. Her 'paramour' as she called him, the man who broke her heart like an egg, became an information technology specialist in Borneo. He set up library systems in jungle portakabins. He married a Brazilian woman who used to be a go-go dancer. I didn't want this information, but Miss Chatham was keen to tell me anyway.

We were sitting in the library tea room. Through the window I could see the Memorial Garden and the chocolate-brown-clad soldier who sits on the memorial to the Unknown Warrior. He has been there as long as I can remember. His uniform looks Great War. He was smoking a cigarette that he had spent five minutes rolling. Miss Chatham confessed that she didn't 'intrude' on My Mother's private affairs and couldn't help me. As far as she could remember there were no 'male companions' at that time.

As I passed through the library I went through the reading room. There was a chocolate-brown-clad tramp in there eating what was left of a vanilla slice from a semi-crushed bakery box. He was also licking the remnants of a chocolate éclair that were crushed on the box lid. He has been there since the afternoon in 1978 when he choked on a Danish pastry he wasn't supposed to be eating.

Ellen Danby lives in America now and Mrs McCann is dead.

That evening I pushed myself back to the Waiting Room. My astral self, still in Technicolor. Mrs Berry was crocheting. It never gets any larger, some tablecloth she's never going to complete. There was another man there now, just coming through the door. He was stopped by the angel on the other side and a few words were exchanged, then he was let through.

'Wait,' I shouted and lurched forward hoping to jam my foot in the door before the angel yanked it shut. I was of course too late. All my energies were focussed on projecting myself there. The angel had endless energy, focussed on the Universe. Shutting an MDF door is a reflex. The man stood there waiting his turn. As the door shut he spoke.

'I was just coming to talk to you,' he said. I was shaking. *Is this him? My Dad?*

'It's about my wife, April. I need you to find her, give her a message…' I looked at him. Glad that this pot-bellied, sweating man was not mine. I moved past him and knocked on the door.

'Tell her I'm dead.' He looked disturbed as I hammered on the door. 'I left her. Two years ago. Went out for a paper, only I decided I'd go and live in Spain.'

I did not get to speak with Mrs McCann. This time the angel did not even open the door and in the end April's husband got edgy that having talked his way out he wouldn't be able to talk his way back in. Finally he told me to go because clearly they weren't opening the door until I had. April's husband got very shirty with me, his voice getting higher pitched. Stranded.

I put April out of her misery. April cried a lot, but they were tears of relief. Of letting go. She would be heading off to the airport soon and was going to be met at the other end by his Spanish widow. It depressed me utterly.

I opened the Bourbon biscuits and then I cold-called Alan

Hartley, who put the phone down on me three times. Then I tried Paul Whelan, who did not remember My Mother. Genuinely so. He was friendly enough, even asking his newest wife if she remembered him ever having mentioned a Madeleine Colville.

There were seven O. Howards in the phone book and I called them all. Only three were men. Of the men, the third one was my Oliver Howard.

'Do you remember a woman called Madeleine Colville?'

'Yes. I'm afraid Madeleine is dead.'

'I know. I'm her daughter. Annie.'

This was met with several moments of silence. I sat at my end thinking that perhaps he was imagining the moment of my conception, some lush and sexy moment of his life that he had always cherished. I thought that he was probably sifting through a catalogue of memories of My Mother at her most beautiful, her most sexy, her most womanly. Madeleine Colville, the love of his life.

'Is that all?' he said very coldly. A man who keeps his voice in the deep freeze.

'Are you my father?'

'I doubt it.'

'You've thought about it then?'

'No.'

'Are you my father?'

'No.'

'Why did you have to use the word "doubt"? Now you've got me thinking. If you doubt it, Mr Howard, that means you must have thought about it. Doesn't it?'

There was another acre of silence then.

'I am not your father. I don't know who your father was. If I am brutally honest Hannah…'

'Annie.'

'Annie…I doubt that your mother knew who your father was.
Do you understand what I am saying? Your mother enjoyed
herself…on a grand scale.'

Now it was my turn to be silent.

'Can I have a list?'

Which is when he put the phone down. He pulled the plug
on it too. I tried the next day and got no response.

So I headed over to his house to see if I could get a personal
response. I knocked on the door. I rang the bell. I waited in the
front garden, sitting on the neatly trimmed grass. Grass that was
neatly trimmed by a gardener.

Mrs Howard was first home. She'd been out at a charity lunch.
Clearly this had exhausted all her charity, as she frogmarched
me down to the gates and made me wait outside. Oliver
Howard's detached Georgian home had large, ornately wrought
iron gates. If you looked at them long enough they could become
even more ornate. At first glance there were branches and leaves.
Then as your eyes traced along the branches you'd find birds,
finches with stubby beaks, here a wren and suddenly a squirrel,
an owl at the very topmost left-hand corner. Finally there were
the bees and the ladybirds and the dragonfly.

Mrs Howard had not done much forward thinking when she
locked the gates behind me. As Oliver Howard arrived home in
his glossy new Rover he had to leave the safety of the vehicle to
talk with her over the intercom. He didn't see me at first beside
the row of hydrangeas on the grass banking.

'What's going on? You've locked me out.'

There was a tinny, clattering response and he looked round.
Looking for me.

'Where?…For Pete's sake Syb I can't see her.'

I moved to stand behind him as he berated her and received

tinny responses. She was safe within the house. She had the power to keep him locked out. He was in the middle of ticking her off, telling her she was a paranoid bag when he stepped back. I was there. Almost under his feet. He hung up the phone as she was in mid-tirade.

'You're Hannah,' he stated, looking tired.

'I'm Annie. I'm just here for a few pointers. I am looking for my dad…'

'No. Not him. Not me.'

'No. I understand. But My Mother is dead and I haven't anyone else I can ask.'

'You can't ask me. I don't know.'

He folded his arms, defensive and yet making himself bigger, top-heavy with sleeves and elbows.

'I thought you might remember someone.'

He looked down then at the gravel under his soft leather shoes. He took a deep breath. Then, speaking from above his elbow-forearm barricade, 'I'm not him. Truly, so help me Godly. I swear on the Bible that I don't have any idea who sired you. Your mother didn't go into details. You were already there when I met her. I will say that I was her first for a long time. You were about eighteen months old I think. You'd stopped her in her tracks. She'd got her figure in shape and she'd picked me out.'

He folded his bottom lip in then, over his teeth as if that finished the matter.

'You didn't stay with her. Why?'

'She didn't stay, Annie. She left me. I'd've married her. Seriously. Even with you in tow. The only woman I've ever wanted to marry.'

His glance slithered to the intercom then, checking that he hadn't accidentally left the frequency open. I could imagine the wife he hadn't wanted to marry listening in to white noise.

'Why did she leave you?'

He shrugged.

'But you came back. Later.'

'Yes. She offered.'

'You didn't marry her then either.'

Now he unfolded the bottom lip and instead folded the top lip behind his bottom teeth and let out an irritated wheezing sound.

'I was already married by then.'

He spoke very quietly and finally and looked at me with a finished expression as if he had just about explained the universe to me and that was that. I looked back, trying to see through his eyes into his memory. To see the true story in all its details. For everything he said simply opened up more gateways, more dirt tracks. A maze. I felt he had so much to give me that he was being mean and stingy keeping all this knowledge to himself.

His wife was tapping down the drive now in her high-heeled beige shoes. Expensive shoes. Ugly shoes. She was triumphant behind the gate, brandishing keys to let him in.

'I've called the police so if you know what's best for you, you won't be here when they arrive.'

Oliver Howard groaned.

'Talk about taking things completely out of all proportion.'

He got back into the car, almost mowing her down as he moved into the drive, driving past her, up to the door. She gaped, angry that he was not going to give her a lift up the drive to the house. I watched her tappety all the way back to the front door. You could almost see the hairs on the back of her neck standing up, knowing that I waited.

I watched. She shut the door. A light went on in a conservatory at the back of the house. I could see one edge of the windows, a sofa, a giant tropical pot plant curling up into the roof. The blinds came down then, like a blink.

There was no use going to his office. The first day he was away in Nottingham. The second day he was out at a business breakfast on the industrial estate and his secretary/assistant/dogsbody called him on the mobile to warn him. He didn't return. He didn't go home. He holed up at the golf club where I was escorted to the gates in a bunker buggy.

On the third day the security guard at his offices wouldn't let me in. He was very polite but very firm despite not being the tallest, bulkiest guard I had ever encountered. He had power because he was thoughtful. What he said and the tone he used were more forceful than if he had physically hoisted me up by my knicker elastic and hurled me into the street.

On the fourth day I sat outside the house finding woodpeckers and peregrine falcons in those gates. I stayed for hours sitting on a low wall. I noticed only that the blinds in the conservatory were drawn. When it grew dark I pulled on a jacket. I had a notion, I don't know what I think about this now, that perhaps the seven-year spell was breaking, ending with madness; my notion was that if I stayed all night I might be able to tune into Oliver Howard's dreams.

If I could just pick up the right frequency I could be inside his dreams, sort through his memories for myself. He wouldn't be harmed, he wouldn't even know I was there. If he did, he would just think it was a dream brought on by our recent encounters. He might spend some of the next morning thinking about me and then he'd have an important meeting scheduled and I would vanish. I could spend the night hours finding out. I could see My Mother before she was My Mother, perhaps when she was a stranger.

I struggled hard after all the lights were out, struggled against the night full of servants and people mown down by horse and carriage, people scarred by smallpox. People I did not want to see or hear. Clutter.

I willed. Strained. Concentrated. Wished.

On the fifth day they called the police.

THE EXTRA LARGE MEDIUM

Detailed Report: Incident number 79845A/Z
Constable Terry Adam

Report on female stalker at home of Oliver
Howard.

What's to report? Shouldn't say it but Mrs Howard
calls us out on a regular basis for nothing at
all. Strange cars parked in the neighbourhood.
Nuisance cats. Prowlers who always turn out to be
surveyors or estate agents dressed in suits and
wielding tape measures and damp meters and
instamatic cameras. The one and only time there
was a break-in Polly Howard didn't know about it
until she read the piece in the local paper. Then
we had a series of abusive calls from her yapping
... Sorry, I'll keep it businesslike, informing us
of her disappointment with our policing and her
dismay at the waste of taxpayers' money.

I'm beyond dismay. I want to raid her house
early morning, bundle her into the back of the
squad car and take her to the estate where the
carpeting, if they have any, sticks to your feet
when you walk on it. Where little kids are
learning the cottage industry of crack cocaine
manufacture. Want to show her the body in the
dumpster at the back of the Drayman's Arms. The
abandoned pensioner. Not everyone lives in a
Georgian mansion, Polly Howard. Stop. Stop.
Breathe.

Historical note: nothing has changed. When the
Howards' house was first built in about 1739 there
was an opium den and a whore house and gin
palaces and no police force. There was a
highwayman, Red Rob, who used to operate
practically outside Polly Howard's front door.
Sorry. Sorry.

Back to the facts. I was in and I volunteered to go up to check on Mrs Howard. I had had a bad morning with a body in the kitchen of a corner house on the estate. Not very old. Bloke. Drugs related. Sniffing Ajax it looked like. Depressing. I try to keep this type of event at arm's length. You have to. It should be in the training. My own personal blocking tactic is to erase the memory of it by filling in a detailed report. That way all the facts are noted, fresh and clear from my head. That way all the facts are flushed out of my head. I've been commended on the quality of my scene-of-crime reporting. I don't want to carry that useless knowledge around. It isn't as if I'm going to find it handy one evening in the pub quiz. That particular day, the report didn't do it. Couldn't get it out of my head. I'd had a restless night the night before (still couldn't shake the recent fatal RTA I'd attended either) and this had lowered my mental defences. This is the reason I volunteered. All right, I confess. I was trying to run away.

I like the Old Park area. It's lush and green and old. Forget the fact that it is Millionaires' Row. The houses are fine. I don't care that there isn't one of them that sells for under half a million these days. I care on an historical level. They are unusual and beautiful and have travelled through time. They have the quirks and delights of their original owners written into the brickwork and stonemasonry. Polly Howard doesn't live there. She inhabits the space. Hezekiah Wheatfield lives there. Not that I believe in ghosts. I mean, his legacy. What he left behind. Whatever. Sorry. Sorry.

I like the Old Park area because the houses

don't impinge on the wildlife. The trees don't
have to fight their way through concrete. In the
park you can see goldfinches and greenfinches, the
odd woodpecker. You can usually hear the
woodpeckers. Jays. The dappled. The speckled.
The light through the copper beech. It is
restful. The trees have space. I thought it would
do me good to have a run up there. Cleanse my
soul.

I do not think that Annie Colville was a
danger to anyone. She was emotionally charged
but by no means hysterical. We talked for some
minutes under the copper beech trees and I
learned that she was looking for her biological
father and had wanted to talk with Mr Howard,
had in fact had some conversations with him
already. I reiterated a point that Mr Howard had
made already it seemed. That point was that he
wasn't her biological parent and didn't know who
was and that there wasn't much point pursuing
him.

But the point is, if you let go, you lose it.

At this juncture I was able to give Annie a
couple of names of people I had had contact with
who help adopted offspring search for their
biological parents. I put her on to Dorothy in
town who is very helpful and sympathetic. Dorothy
reads a lot of mystery fiction and quite frankly
could do a lot better than a couple of our
detectives. She's an eye for details. She's got
excellent people skills. If she couldn't
find anyone for Annie she would at the very least
be able to make her feel better about the
situation. Annie Colville listened and she put up
no resistance to being moved on. She looked tired
and I was relieved she accepted a lift back into

town in the squad car.

I took the longest route. I could lie and say
that I did this to give her time to gather her
thoughts. I did it because I wanted to keep her
in the car with me for just a few more moments.
Up through the furthest edges of the park along
the perimeter walling of Rood House. Past the
boating lake. Along the river. Following the
river back into town, across the bridge. I took
that route because there was something about
her.

I wanted to take her in my arms. Hold her. At
the roadside, under the copper beech tree I
wanted to hoist her up and carry her off. It
isn't allowed is it? Eh? That is one advantage of
horses over cars. If you're going to give a woman
a lift on your horse you have to lift her up. You
have to make physical, human contact. Her body
neatly spooned against yours in the saddle. Your
arms encircling her waist to hold the reins. We
are too far apart in modern times.

Not that I'll do anything about this. Not that
I can ever bring myself to say anything, to even
ask the woman out for something as basic as a
drink because I can't be taken on. The baggage
would weigh anyone down. I know it weighs me
down.

On the way home I drove past the Howards'
place. Mrs Polly Howard was impressed with my
follow-up procedure. Annie had not been back.

Job done.

Forget it. Time for a brew. Time to scrumple
this up and start again. Make a fresh copy. Facts
only this time.

Interview with self: suspended @ 19.27

Viewed from the bridge

ISAMBARD KINGDOM Brunel did not build this suspension bridge. Sir Charles Whitworth wanted him to, arranged a special meeting, travelled to London taking a few town bigwigs with him. They took the photographer, Guild. The Guild family still have a photography studio in our town.

Isambard Kingdom Brunel died that morning. He didn't do this on purpose but Sir Charles Whitworth took it as a personal slight and vowed they would build a bigger, more modern bridge than Brunel could have designed. Or engineered, I don't know. What do you do with bridges?

They have Guild's photographs of the construction work in the library archive. There had been a ferry up until then. He made a few thousand taking people on construction viewing trips and kept the ferry going for the squeamish or 'those of a nervous disposition' who couldn't hack going over the bridge. It is very high, spanning the top of one side of the valley straight across to the other. The sides were too steep to run a road up to the top. The bridge had to go up and across, not just simply across. From Old Road to Red Rob Road.

Red Rob being the highwayman whose pitch this was before the bridge. Before Sir Charles Whitworth. Before photographs. He's stuffed in the museum, believe it or not. He hangs in a glass case with the curtains drawn to keep the daylight from destroying him. Like a vampire. You have to go under the curtain and press a button. Then a dim light illuminates his tanned face, his dead, glass eyes looking out at you, the faintest trace of bristle just under his nose. The ultimate bogeyman. He looks tanned brown because of the preservatives he is soaked in. Skin is, after all, simply pale pink leather.

There are two Gothic-style towers at each end that used to be for tolls. Eventually someone realised that the bridge's construction had cost so much they would never pay back the debt. Now we pay a set amount each year in our council tax for the upkeep of the bridge. They even call it the Bridge Tithe. There are three men who paint and maintain it endlessly, dangling from cradles, abseiling up and under like spiders. Now they have specialist cabling and technology. When Sir Charles Whitworth commissioned the bridge they didn't. They built it with sweat and hammering. They were hauled up and down hemp lines in oversized buckets.

Which is why, as I stood leaning over the balustrading looking into the river, three chocolate-brown-clad workmen were sitting just underneath me. They were perched like birds on the iron angled girder below the deck. I could hear their chat and smell the tobacco as they smoked into the night.

'Don't see the boats so much now,' said a stocky bearded one, scratching at his chin like a flea-ridden dog.

'The steam packet runs.' The thin one is leaning into the

girder, stretching himself along its length. He looks like a masthead on a ship, his form bent to the metal. At one with the girder.

'To the tea garden and back.' A wiry bloke on haunches, pinching his cigarette out. 'Don't go nowhere else now.' Tossing it. It arced like a diver, to the water below.

'All right. I'll give you the steam packet. But not the tugs and the fireboat and the little cargo barges.'

'No. But the carriages look pretty in the night, with their lights.'

They pondered the roadways on either side for a moment. Looked down into town and the shift and glide of headlights.

'What happened to the horses? You don't never see the horses.' The stocky man adjusted his position, resting one foot higher up the girder, leaned a hairy arm on his leg, relaxed.

'Ate them. Or shipped them off on those bloody little cargo barges...' The wiry man grinned, winked and they all chuckled.

'You jumping or what?' Wiry spoke up, tilting his head so that he could look straight up at me through a gap in the decking. I looked back. Unsure of the answer.

'She's here for the view.' The stocky one was calm, as if this was the sole reason anyone used the bridge.

'It is a beautiful view.' Watching the lights of the cars down to the left where town started. A single car rolled over the bridge behind me, over onto Red Rob Road travelling across the topmost edge of the land like a beacon. The sky was lit with a deep grey-blue. The air was cool. I breathed in.

'We like it.' The tall man shut his eyes as if he was going to snooze. Roost up there.

'Don't you want to be somewhere else? Move on now?' I ventured.

'She's on about Heaven.' Wiry was clearly the cynic.

'No,' said Stocky, squinting into the distance as if he could just make out the sea. 'This is home.'

It was a four-letter word, Home, and it did not seem, at that moment, to apply to me. If I shifted myself over the handrail, if I lifted my leg, hiked myself over the balustrade and let go, where would I end up? Would that be Home? I'd be cosy in my chocolate brown skirt and woolly jumper. Wouldn't I? Isn't that where My Mother was…waiting?

I looked down, although you'd think the path to Heaven should, ideally, be up. Never have had a sense of direction.

As I lifted my leg over the rail I realised the balustrade was higher than it had seemed. I was half on, half off, my feet suddenly no longer in contact with the decking but my middle, my hands, flat on the handrail. Clinging on. It seemed that down continued for a very long way. The river didn't seem like a river, it was more like a vast well. If I jumped, probably, about an hour from now, there would be a faint splash rustling in the bottom of the valley.

And then I realised how stupid it would be. With my endless back catalogue of unfinished business I'd spend an eternity plunging down, repeating the same tomfoolery over and over in front of the three workmen.

Only now of course I was losing my balance. I was going to slip to my doom in a half-arsed accident, a disgraceful skidding, with no double-twisting pike or triple salko. Which was when I felt my body lurch to a halt, my chin scrape against wrought iron metalwork, felt my shoulder pop out. I thought I had caught my sleeve in the balustrading, saved myself by default. Something held me there.

I looked back. It was Joe, the wrestler. His arm was reaching through the widest part of the balustrading, his hand was clenched around my left arm and beads of sweat were sparkling on his face. His features were twisted up with the effort of it. We were held there for a moment in a stalemate. He couldn't lift me. He could just hold on. I hung there for one of those hour-long minutes that my life is dotted with.

I saw the lights in town, heard a joke car horn *parrump-parp-parp* as it tootled through the Old Park area. Then I reached in and clutched at the decorative iron work.

In the tollbooth on the townward side of the bridge, Joe patched me up with a medical kit, stretching the sticking plaster too tight over my wounded chin. He was shaking. Angry. He didn't say much. The stripping sound of the sticking plaster as he unravelled it. The steely snip of the scissors. The kettle hissing to a boil, now rattling and shushing on his antique stove.

'If you jump you take others with you. Always. Remember that, however depressed you get. You aren't finishing anything. Not for the people left behind.'

He turned to make tea, stirring leaves in a huge shiny brown earthenware pot.

His eyes were less certain however as he offered an old-fashioned biscuit barrel loaded with shortbread. No Bourbons thankfully.

'Think on.'

We thought about it. I told him everything then. It took the entire barrel of biscuits and some cheese on toast. Joe's theory was that Sam would miss me or at the very least be touched, might blame himself. He decided that it sounded as if Brian clearly had problems of his own in the grief department.

He didn't give advice or lecture. It was more of a crossword solution. Three down Evan disappears. Five across My Mother dies. Seven down, the mental strain of waiting seven years for Evan Bees starts to strain your seams a bit, because you are human after all. Five across, your friends at the Spiritualist

Church are dropping hints you should go. Then go. No sense brewing up all this emotional wind.

Joe's phrase. Not mine. Joe also mentioned spells. The ritual of waiting. The mystical capabilities of the number seven.

I did not tell him that I was Annie Colville and that I spoke to the Dead. Didn't want to scare him.

But I sat there for a while with Joe, partly because I didn't really have anywhere to go and he looked like he needed the company. He had a cosy place there, a nest he'd made, roosting as he was so high above the rest of us.

I had taken very little with me from the shed to the Zion Chapel, essentially because I didn't have more. My earthly possessions were dwindling.

I still clung to the handsewn patchwork quilt I'd acquired during my allotment shed days. There was a silver filigree bangle that had belonged to My Mother in a square box. There was a fruit peeling knife she had kept in her handbag at all times. Useful not just for peeling fruits but also for unfastening jammed locks in public toilets. I had another pair of shoes, a change of clothes. A sweater. A petrol blue sweater. A cup, saucer and plate from my shed days, and the teapot.

Other mementos of my sojourn at the shed were in everyday use by Atalanta at The Glade. I didn't need the Swedish stove. That was now at The Glade too. I was beginning to think there were not-so-subtle hints about where I should settle. About where Home was.

It seemed to get dark early and stay dark. I noticed that Joe was getting edgy, looking out of the window, checking the fire in the small Victorian grate. It was getting very cold no matter how many logs he placed there. Joe was looking at me. Expectant. His wristwatch alarm beeped in a panic and startled him. He consulted the time and switched on some more lamps. The bulb popped in one and he began to fumble about in a cupboard, with what I wanted to call desperation.

I've never been fond of the dark. I like to keep a light on. This is my territory, the land of light and I stake a claim.

Sam always thought it was silly and switched it off before plunging into a sleep as deep as the ocean. A transcontinental express train with a brass band on board could have driven through our bedroom at the speed of sound and not even the sonic boom would have woken him. There were many nights when I got up and slept in the even boxier, aptly named, box room with the light on.

I think it is something I inherited from My Mother. She always kept the lights on. One in my room, and one on the landing and a small bedside one in her room. There was even the mail-order million candlepower emergency torch she kept by her bed.

She smiles at me. In the past. She didn't think at the time that the memory of it would break my heart but it does. I don't really remember her face. The feeling of love and safety, of being there with her is more vivid. But I don't see it in total focus. It is the CCTV of memory.

Then I thought about Evan Bees and once again what I saw was the empty chair at the table that first night alone. The place I set for him. The knife and fork unmatched. A washed-out spot of tomato sauce on the placemat, the smell of spaghetti catching in the dried-out pan.

I left the place setting where it was for a month. I made spaghetti with every sauce I could think of each night. Carbonara on Tuesday. Tomato and basil on Wednesday. Pesto on Thursday. Garlic and pancetta on Friday. At the weekends, eventually, I started to help out full time at The Glade and ate there.

After I made spaghetti with custard I put the place setting

away and only ate in the living room, balancing a plate on my knees. I have never eaten spaghetti since.

It was nearly two-thirty in the morning when they started to arrive. Joe, I realised, had prepared. A breeze started up. Joe pulled on a heavy wool donkey jacket, took a deep breath, said simply, 'Here come the Night Shift.'

He couldn't see them, he could only feel them and hear the way they banged about the architecture. The rattling door, the books slammed from the shelves. Footsteps running up and down his spiral staircase. And the extreme of cold. The smells. Every night this happened to him at two-thirty. I think two-thirty is the optimum time. Most people, in my hemisphere at least, are asleep. The barriers are down now. We all inhabit other worlds, dream worlds, the Land of Nod, Hypnos. I seem to inhabit the Underworld. In they came in their chocolate brown clothing, bitter chocolate in the case of those who'd actually jumped into the river. Sodden. Dripping. Chilled.

It was noisy in there. They didn't crowd each other so much as forget anyone else existed. I looked at Joe who was ashen, his face sweating. He looked ill but he only glanced at me and shrugged. They were making him ill, their presence.

There was an intensity in what they had to say which surprised me. You'd think that someone who decides to jump off a bridge would say all they had to say, leave a note. Write a list.

Evidently not. Much of it is garbled.

'Like 'at see? He is, in 'e? 'Xactly like that. So catch 'im and tell 'im eh?'

'And he goes about. And he goes about.'

'Tall. Just tall. You'll know him. Tall. Like a tree. Tall. Thin. Bit of a pot round the middle and his hair's parted like this…' Strange wavy gesture over head.

It was like being tuned to all the radio stations at once and you have no idea what anyone is talking about.

Then there were the others. Victims of highway robbery bleeding pure chocolate sauce. The gallows men and women left to rot in the woods on Red Rob Road. They come wailing and ranting and declaring vengeance or curses or innocence.

'The magistrate, Newbold, what's become of him?'

The sensible question sailed out of the storm of words and I spun round. A man in a swagger coat and a tricorn hat looking impatient. It was difficult to read what he wanted. Did he want the magistrate to have died of some lingering illness or had he planned on one of his confederates bumping him off? I took too long to think about it. He started haranguing me then. Others pushed forward and he grew angry. He stepped into me, a pain in my neck, a suffocated, crushing feeling in my chest as he shouted and shouted his innocence through my lips.

I don't know where they went after I fainted.

In the Land of the Giant, Brian:
forest

The first time she comes to tell me Annie is looking for her father and has got into difficulty. Atalanta is very kind about this. She avoids the use of the word 'trouble'. She mentions the police and is calm about it. She wants to know if I have any information. If I could help Annie.

Now I wish that Maddie had told me everything. That I had more to think about, that my memory did not have limits and boundaries. I don't try and imagine what Maddie was like before I knew her. That is just making it up. Before long I will not be able to remember the truth. I hold on tightly to what I have.

I explain my situation to Atalanta. That it is my fault. That I did not want Maddie to relive her past history simply because it was past. I did not think about Annie.

Annie is at the Spiritualist Church most evenings. I don't ask Atalanta outright but somehow she guesses what I am thinking. Maddie has never come back with a message. Atalanta thinks this is a problem for Annie. That she is waiting, just as she has waited for her husband to return. We talk for a long time.

She comes to tell me news. I know that she comes to see me and that news of Annie is simply our excuse. We don't have to say it out loud that I look forward to her arriving. That on the mornings that I know she will be arriving I make a cup of tea and I stand in the window. I cannot sit. If I sit I might miss that first view of her head as she climbs the path. When she comes through the trees.

I wish now that I had something to give to Annie. In return.

Lost is found

I WOKE UP hours later in a small curl under the donkey jacket. Aching in every muscle, most especially the ones in my neck. Other than that there was no evidence of what happened. Even Joe was whistling as he brewed more tea, toasted more cheese.

Something had changed for me. I asked Joe for pen and paper and wrote down whatever details I could remember. Names. Places. I knew exactly how these people felt. I had felt the same as I stood outside Oliver Howard's house. Desperate and isolated. I think the phrase My Mother would use is 'all at sea'. Rolling around on an uncertain flooring, liable to vomit at a given moment.

I asked Joe a simple question.

'Why do you stay here, in this job? Why put up with it every night?'

Joe shrugged.

'It's my responsibility to be here. I can't help that it's haunted.'

Sidney was right. There was no getting away from this and as far as I could see the person who needed help here was Joe and the only person who could help him was me.

I visited the library and asked Miss Chatham for assistance. She was far too busy and put me onto her assistant Lara Crouch. An expert it turned out. My second friend. Lara. Who spent part of her lifetime travelling in the wills and deeds and documents of the town archive.

I began with the magistrate, Newbold. I described the clothes the man had been wearing so Lara could find a proper timescale. I did not tell her straight off, look I've had this experience with a dead man with some heavyweight unfinished business. Instead I made out it was a project for the magistrates' court. That I was a researcher.

It turned out that the widow of the hanged man had married Newbold the magistrate. I blurted out, frustrated, 'I can't tell him that.'

Lara looked at me for a long moment. Actually 'look' is utterly inadequate. What she did was consider me for a good while. I had had little sleep the night before. I was edgy. Tearful even. What was the point in being able to talk to people like this if I was stymied at every opportunity to help them? To sort their deaths out. Where was my easy answer? Where was my way out? Way forward.

'You're Annie Colville.' She sounded relieved, said it in such a quiet, het-up sort of voice. I nodded, expecting to be turfed out of the library.

She took me to another basement. The basement basement. She walked me along a very narrow corridor to a wall of Dewey catalogue drawers. They'd been stored there after the computers had been installed. Partly because Miss Chatham had thought they should have a paper back-up to the cybernetic nonsense. Partly because she couldn't bear to see the beautiful oak cabinets destroyed.

They were beautiful. They had history. They had a ghost.

Lara explained that every day something came to the Dewey catalogue and sorted through, looking for something. Each day there would be drawers left open or cards taken out and left to one side. On other occasions Lara thought she'd seen someone walking along the corridor. Other times she simply felt the hairs on the back of her neck prickle. Doors opened and closed.

'What do you do? You put the cards back?' I asked.

Lara nodded.

'Has it happened today?'

Lara nodded.

'What was on the cards?'

Lara did not nod. Again, she considered. Seemed to me even the least curious person might glance at the cards to see what was written on them. What books were listed.

The books were ones that had been long sold. Old volumes from the twenties. A little research told us of Mr Cambridge, who had worked at the library throughout the twenties after returning home from the Great War shellshocked. I thought then that we couldn't do anything about Mr Cambridge. He was a Mrs Berry—the school of perpetual unfinished business. I told Lara it was most likely that he'd just hang around forever filing and unfiling long-defunct books. This was his loop and if he wasn't doing any harm could she learn to live with him?

Lara didn't know. And then, of course, I met him.

Sometimes you do not want to go. You do not want to meet up

again with friends who will find out that you lived to be an old man.
That you lived to see another war. Sometimes you are afraid because
in your sight you failed others, you weren't strong. You punish yourself.
You hide. You are safe and that is enough.

I struggled to the surface. Down the long narrow corridor
with Lara hurrying behind me. 'What did he say? What did he
say?' I pushed out through the revolving doors into the daylight.
Car fumes and music playing in the shop across the road. At the
church opposite there was a wedding, people dressed up, a filmy
veil and flowers. They stood amongst the gravestones and they
could not see the crowd of chocolate-brown-clothed people
watching the wedding.

That night at the Tollbooth tower I told Newbold's story to
the man in the tricorn hat. Newbold had married his widow not
too long after the hanging. They had stayed married for twenty
years or more, until Newbold died. They had had seven children,
all of whom survived to adulthood.

I had expected him not to be pleased at this, to rant about the
unfaithfulness of his wife. But instead it satisfied him. His wife
had been taken care of. Newbold had made good on the injus-
tice. He tipped his hat and departed.

Which left me with several others ranting and agitated. I
checked down the list of facts and figures that I had researched
with Lara at the library. Newspaper stories, obituaries, probate
records.

I told everyone to shut up. I wanted to send a message back
this time, and I was going to do it. They were all to go back and
request that someone send friends to collect Mr Cambridge. If
they didn't do this, I wouldn't help them.

But they shouted and they ranted and they wouldn't listen.
I sat, in true customer-service-desk style, weary of the complaints

at last. I sat there unsmiling and nodded at the information, however piecemeal and cryptic it was.

Tell them to send someone.

They did.

Dig Deep with Arthur:
with a soft brush

Evan Bees spent the night in the bike shed.

He looked like the bike shed was actually five-star accommodation compared to what he'd recently been used to. He was wasted, skinny by nature, made more so by having to forage in bins. There are scientists who have proved now that bears out in Alaska who forage for junk food and our leftovers produce bigger, healthier cubs who survive more easily and grow into bigger, healthier adult bears. They do it on a diet of Budweiser and KFC. It is a scientific fact.

Evan Bees wasn't an Alaskan bear. Although the way Bridget looked at him the next morning when he claimed his spot in the trench you'd have thought he was. His hair was greasy and very long. He looked as if he'd just let it grow like a weed. She gave him the job because she was desperate for the help. She stuck him in the furthest trench on the dig so we couldn't smell him. No one spoke to him.

He didn't travel back with us in the minibus either. One minute he was there. The next he was gone and Bridget was heaving a sigh of relief.

But he hadn't done a runner. He had gone into town to the barber's and had a scalper. He'd also invested in a wet shave. The barber was chuffed to bits, a chance to show off one of his skills. No one asked for a wet shave anymore on account of Gillette and that man who bought the company.

So Evan Bees comes back for dinner looking very clean and tidy but even skinnier. He's bought clothes at the charity shop, two carrier bags full. He's struggled to find the right sizes, jeans and pants that bit too short, sweaters that bit too big.

He burns his other clothes. When he thinks no one is looking. I am having a smoke sitting on the recycled wood garden chairs behind the old coal shed. I watch Evan. I watch his ritual burning. I watch him cry.

He feels comfortable in someone else's clothes. He likes the feel of his shorn hair, running his hand across the stubbled wasteland of his hairline, relaxed, enjoying the sensation. Bridget tries him out, runs her hand across his cropped scalp. He doesn't pull away. But he doesn't like it.

In the first few evenings he is distant, settling himself with a few volumes from the shelves, flicking through a botanical dictionary and *My First Book of Harrier Jump Jets*. Bridget offers him wine which he accepts, although she doesn't get any conversation in return. And she tries.

She sees someone shy and intellectual. I see someone hiding.

On the second morning he takes himself off to the furthest trench again and stays there all day. At lunch he takes his sandwiches and he distances himself again. He is intent. Concentrated. His work is meticulous and he comes up with some good finds. I look over the beads and the buckles as he catalogues them at the end of the day. He has taken a lot of good notes. Mapped everything to the last millimetre.

What I see when I look in the trench is a man digging himself out.

He isn't into cards but he likes wine. He has his ritual glass in the evening. He makes a friend for life, a sexual favour just waiting to be called in, when he buys Bridget a bottle of wine at the end of the first week. She thinks she's on a winner for the weekend.

No. He drinks his single glass with the spaghetti carbonara that Andy has cooked for us all. Then he heads out.

He has not gone to the pub. We all arrive there later and he is not to be found. He comes back too late, the doors are locked up, and spends another night in the bike shed. On Saturday he is gone all day, comes home very tired but invigorated. He takes his boots off in the boot room. The scent of his socks permeates every room. It is moments like that that you wish you'd read more

Conan Doyle and could work out just how far a man has walked by the smell of his feet.

He is allocated a room with me and Andy. He has to have the lower bunk because the first night he falls out of the top bunk. It's fortunate that Andy is a slob and has left an open suitcase of clothes in the path of his fall. Evan Bees does not have a suitcase. He just has his carrier bags. He folds the clothes neatly and stores them under his bed in a cardboard fruit box he found in the kitchen.

It is like I said. Who needs television when you have a real-life mystery like Evan Bees unfolding before your eyes? And the joy of Evan Bees is that you have to work at the story because he is telling you nothing.

It is five days before we get his name. He tells us he is Mike Harsfeld. At least he does the first time Andy asks outright. Mike Harsfeld. But later when he doesn't answer to Mike he covers over his blunder by telling us he is in fact, Mark. Bridget and Andy and the others don't bat an eyelid. They assume they misheard his name. That is in fact what he tells them, says it several times over as a joke, trying to hypnotise them into believing him. Succeeding.

Not me. I know that he is not Mike. He is not Mark. He is not Harsfeld. Harsfeld is the name on the label of his charity-shop sweater. Some cheapo Swedish brand. It is hanging out of his collar and I can read it clearly.

He settles on Mark Harsfeld. The next day he has cut the label from his sweater.

I am the only person who sees that for the first three weeks he is in the hostel Evan Bees/Mark/Mike/Whoever, sleeps under the bed. Andy who sleeps above him never notices. He simply slithers out of his own bunk and into the shower rooms each morning. Andy does not officially wake up until he gets out into the fresh air.

At first glance you'd think the bunk was just empty, recently vacated by someone eager for their early morning pee. I see Evan under the bed. I take my time getting my washbag and my towel and I leave and give Evan the time to scuttle out. To get his washbag. To pretend to the world that he sleeps in a bed like the rest of us.

I miss the catalyst that allows him to sleep in the bed. I just wake up one morning early. It is one of those moments when you are simply wide awake even though it is only half past five in the morning. I can't really move about since there are two other blokes in here to disturb. Although I am lying there thinking that Andy sleeps like the dead and Evan is under the bed and shielded.

I am just reaching for my smokes and making a move towards the kitchen when I hear Evan mumbling. I look round and there he is at last, on the mattress instead of on the floor underneath. He is twisted into the envelope sheets they give you. I have long since been out and bought my own sheets. Evan is knotted into his, trussed in sleep.

What I hear him mumble is, 'Catalogue it for me, Annie. Annie?' I watch him for a moment as his sleeping legs struggle against the sheeting and then I move to the kitchen for a solitary pot of tea. Solitary is not something you can do well in a hostel with a group of archaeologists. I have always been solitary. Now I simply snatch the moments and they are the more savoury to me because I have to work at them.

In this solitary moment I look out through the barrack-room-style metal windows, overpainted and overpainted through the years. I see a skylark in the topmost branch of a tall tree just beyond our huts. I can see that Martin is standing having his solitary moment outside the kitchen. He is eating a bread roll and looking at the skylark through his binoculars. So I stop looking out and intruding on his solitary time. I head out to the recycled garden furniture with my pot of tea and a couple of reheated pastries from yesterday. The microwave pings like a ruddy church bell at this time in the morning.

Outside it is fresh and sunny and I sit and I wonder who Annie is.

Look out

I WAS PERSONA non grata at the Spiritualist Church. It had deteriorated beyond simply not knowing how to tell me to go. They didn't bar the doors or hang garlic from the windowpanes, but they did not put the kettle on. They requested that I cut my sessions to Thursdays only. And then only alternate Thursdays. As I stepped up to the platform several people stepped out. I was scary again. A Midwich Cuckoo once more.

I wish now they had hung onto me tighter. By sheer force of will they might have assisted me later. Like changing channels on the television so you don't have to see the sex, hear the bad language, witness the violence. I couldn't change channels. I was jammed on Red Hot and Dead.

I moved out of Zion Chapel and, in a feeble attempt at settling, took the lease on a basement flat/workshop/office. The basement office was in Old Town. It had to be. I was drawn there. It couldn't be Dollyville or the sixties concrete nightmare of the old shopping precinct.

To be honest, anyone first going through the door would say it was a damp cellar and that to call it office space was fiction. I didn't care. The second the letting agent opened the door and I got a whiff of mildew I felt at home. More at home than I had felt for a long time. There was nothing inside. Old floorboards, a dead pigeon in the grate. A smell of cats. Ancient newspapers littering the floor where they had just taken up a mouldering carpet that was sitting rolled up outside in the yard.

I signed the contract within an hour. I took it for a year at first. I had plans to buy eventually. Don't ask why. It is one of life's unanswerables. I haunted the basement, living like a troll those first few weeks. I spent evenings listening to the street, watching the feet go trip-trapping past or hearing footsteps and missing the passer-by.

At long last I realised it was not a passer-by. It was a haunter-in. She was always late for work. Hanging her chocolate brown scarf on a no-longer-extant hook. I think her dress was most probably a dull brown when she was alive. She was a maid. Scullery. Parlour. Whatever, she was always late.

What was I doing there?

Yes. OK. I'm lying. I know exactly what I was doing.

I was settling into a pit.

It was a newspaper advertisement that showed me my escape route and my way forward. All that lifesaving information in the For Sale columns.

I decided that finding the Lost would help me and perhaps help others along the way. It seemed this had been shouting in my ear for a long time only I had misheard it. Evan Bees was my first big hint. I should have gone out and looked for him. But then, I expected him to return. There is something of failure in the admission that he did not want to be with me. He wanted to run away. Abandon me.

I bought secondhand office furniture, quite ready to accept its ghosts. I cleaned up and then I paid a visit to the police station to talk to someone about setting up my 'bureau'. It was only going to be on a local scale. You could check in with the police, the National Missing Persons Helpline. Then, when those possibilities were exhausted there would be me. The last resort. Pop in on your way out of the police station.

I was going to call it—did, in fact, call it—the LookOut. I was trying to convey that sense of hope and expectation. Being 'on the lookout' for someone implies their return. Missing Persons Bureau implies they are missing. Vanished. Gone.

The police station was built in the 1920s and was a red brick toytown-looking place. You half expected Noddy, Big Ears and Mr Plod to come out of the revolving doors. Inside it was rather cramped and painted gloss cream. The light shone in at strange angles through the tiny square panes of green glass and reflected off the gloss. Shards of light caught you in the eyes, startling and unsettling. I had to look at the desk sergeant cock-eyed to avoid the glare of the morning sun.

Not that he was the desk sergeant, not since he'd been shot in the town's first ever bank robbery in 1932. They had never caught the three robbers who would all have suffered the death penalty. Hence Sergeant Laidlaw's presence in his old station. Unfinished business.

As I waited for a living officer Detective Inspector Knight came out of a side door. He looked harassed.

'I'll be back at one Dixie. Dixie?'

He leaned past me, gave me a querying look as if I had perhaps eaten Dixie. Then, remembering me, said, 'What do you want?' which seemed to be his standard greeting. He gave me a hard stare and I was struck that he didn't want to know what I had to say. He didn't want a message. He was scared of me, still.

I mentioned my idea, finding the living as well as the Dead, only I didn't put it quite like that. To my surprise he nodded and said, 'Get the buggers off our backs.'

He said he'd put me onto one of their Community Liaison Officers. Take a seat.

What I got was Terry Adam.

He had me signed up and labelled as a crank after our encounter at, as he put it, 'the Howard residence'. Still, credit to the man, he was patient with me. He let me look over some of the official paperwork forms that they fill in. Personally I think that they had overstocked and he was simply shifting the burden of recycling paper. He seemed very keen on his forms and reports and paperwork.

I looked over the form. It asked the bare minimum. You were left with a badly patched photofit of the missing person. In fact, you missed them utterly. It was no wonder they never seemed to find anyone. Not that I mentioned this to Terry Adam. He looked empty and hard and emotionless, as though if you leaned over and rapped on his head with your knuckles there would be a hollow sound inside, tinny and cold.

He mentioned my quest for Dad just before I took my leave and it made me edgy, as if he was looking right into me, like a narrow searchlight, someone shining a bright torch through your letterbox. It was not often that the living did this to me. Terry Adam reminded me of the name he'd given me, the counsellor, Dorothy Cromwell. He reached into a small drawer and got out her business card. Handed me a couple, 'In case you lose one.' And I felt rapped on the knuckles somehow. He said she was a good listener and might be able to help.

He had a quiet voice, insistently so. He didn't seem to listen to anything I had to say, he just decided matters. He was not taking me seriously I could tell. He was not going to let me help him and he was not going to help me. Except in the way he saw fit. He knew that I was trying to cling to my bit of wood from the wreckage at this point, but Terry Adam, he seemed like the kind of person to look over the side and bash you with an oar.

Feeling bullied a bit, I did contact Dorothy. She was a good listener and she helped, if nothing else, to prepare me for what was going to happen when Evan was declared legally dead. Other than that she didn't hold out much hope of ever finding my dad. After all I had no name. No contact of any kind.

She put some details of mine down on a form she had. She smiled, very sympathetic and rather patronising. I thought that Terry Adam had probably rung ahead and warned her that he was sending a crazy stalkerwoman to see her. Humour her. Do the paperwork.

It was my encounter with Pauline Dart that made me think of changes. Made me think what people needed. What they didn't need was paperwork people like Terry Adam. I had only just got going. I had filled in a few forms, because I felt that was what people expected, that without the reality of a bit of ink and some dotted lines the world would tumble out of orbit.

Mostly what people had to say was, 'He's so tall, so fat and he's so loud. Have you seen him? He goes around with that red-haired chap from the chippy.'

It was all dates and heights, the cardboard cutouts of the people. Until Pauline Dart.

Pauline Dart shook me. She came to the LookOut as her last stop. Pauline's sister had gone missing nearly ten years ago after a broken relationship. She was legally dead, but Pauline was hanging onto her. Would not give her up. Pauline had paid a detective for two years to try and find her sister. The detective, a smartly dressed woman who gave breakfast brunch meetings to the local bigwigs and businessmen, had found nothing. She hadn't really looked.

Pauline presented me with a box of keepsakes. She had gone through all her sister's belongings over a two-year period and she had picked out what few things she felt were secret or unusual. She had chosen her clues.

There was a key, a Yale key that did not fit any locks that she knew, certainly none in her sister's house. There was a ticket for a watch repair and the watch. It was something masculine and not familiar at all to Pauline Dart. There was a pebble that she had looked up in the geology section at the university library. It was a particular kind of rock, only found on the Norfolk coast.

This was both puzzling and hopeful to Pauline. She couldn't remember one instance when they had been to Norfolk, not as children, not as adults. Even when Pauline's sister was married, before her divorce, they had never set foot in Norfolk. Pauline had held out a long time on the hope that her sister Fran was living somewhere in Norfolk.

The last straw with the lady detective had been an abortive trip to Cromer. Pauline had been unable to go and she felt that the detective had not looked quite hard enough. There were a lot of people living in Norfolk who had received strange telephone calls from Pauline Dart asking if they would help. Had they seen this woman, so tall, so dark, so thin?

There was a piece of gold gift ribbon from a box of Thornton's chocolates. There was a button, black, polished, made of some shell rather than plastic. A foreign coin, a Dutch guilder. From when there still were Dutch guilders. The discarded head from an electric toothbrush. A tube of lipstick in a shade that was unusual for Fran. A pocket mirror with a painted, dragonfly back. A brown paper bag folded neatly bearing no markings except a small, pencilled addition 10+63+8 in the top corner.

Pauline had spent three months tracing the origins of that bag, discovering it was for greengrocery rather than sweets, or possibly a bakery bag. She had trawled shops looking at prices to find out what might have cost 10+63+8.

What Pauline Dart did was keep her sister with her. What she did was invent a secret life. A life still to be lived. A life where Fran was different and new and happy. Now Pauline was nearing the end of the shoebox. She was approaching the gates of grief, tall and squeaking. The gates that trap your fingers.

What I did was pick up the thread for her and keep spinning. She could get on with life, save her own marriage which had been creaking under the detective work, the obsessive compulsion. I asked her what Fran's favourite colour was. How she brewed tea, or if she preferred coffee. I asked about sayings and foibles. The day-to-day. The details.

Who you are is not in your hair colour or the size of your feet. Who you are is in your rituals and your pet hates.

After Pauline left, the shoebox sat on my secondhand office desk. I realised that I had almost nothing of Evan. We were not, as I've said, great photographers. We didn't travel much even for day trips and we never remembered the camera. Thinking, I couldn't remember ever having one. My Mother was not a camera person much. It is a learned thing I think. Now it seemed I had moved away from Evan. I had kept nothing except my memories and my feelings.

As I looked through Pauline's shoebox at the fragments of Fran, I was pierced by the thought that many of the memories I now had of Evan were his absence. The empty chair. The dried-out teacup. His space in the bed. And all these empty spaces had been lost to me as I became an empty space myself. The troll in the basement.

I dug out my only photo of Evan that night and I photocopied it onto a ream of white paper. The more I looked at the image the less familiar he became. His photocopied face took precedence.

By midnight I had drawn a beard and moustache on a few. On others I had drawn curly hair or pigtails.

Next morning found me cutting out hairstyles and hats from magazines and sticking them on Evan's image. Manufacturing a new improved Evan, the Evan he might have wanted to be. A stranger.

Dig Deep with Arthur:
earwig

I was raised by my gran. My parents were very much in love with each other. Besotted. Passionate. Intertwined. I was in their way. I cramped their style.

Don't get me wrong, I don't resent this one bit. If you could hear my voice you'd know. All I'm doing is laying down some facts for you which I think are relevant. Facts and events that tell you why I searched for her. Facts that inform you as to why it was meant to be.

I nearly didn't exist. In a legal sense. My parents, racked by the trauma of childbirth, didn't register my arrival. There's some time limit and then, young as you are, you go off the official list. You are a non-person. Don't know what that entails. Being chucked out of public libraries, hunted down by crack squads of illegal-baby trappers.

My parents thought childbirth separated them. It was something, however much Dad got involved, that Mum had to do alone. I have no idea if you've ever had a child. All I can say is that Mum felt that since I was sucking at her breasts all day she did not relish Dad sucking them all night. I was the nadir of their relationship. If they could have been arsed to register me that is what they'd've called me.

Gran did it. Called me Arthur after my grandad. Took me home. Took me out of their way. Took me to her heart. A big, spacious, warm place to live. Get me?

Gran got me up and running quick. I could read and write before school, albeit in an old-fashioned hand taught to me by Gran. I could do mental maths, read a gas bill, check the electricity meter, change a fuse, translate bus and train timetables, cook, sew and knit. Gran had a set regime of life essentials, your kit to get you through.

Her theory was that she was already into her seventies and needed to impart a lot of practical knowledge fairly quickly in case she died sooner than later. Chiefly she taught me independence. Confidence. Unconditional love. Card games.

I'm not saying we didn't have fun. That was on her list too.

Fairytales. Singing. Gran was Irish on her mother's side and had a huge repertoire of alternately morbid and bawdy songs.

She taught me how to read people. How to listen to what isn't being said. She called it earwigging.

Evan Bees, or Mark Harsfeld as he was calling himself at that point, was an earwigger's dream. I worked out fairly quickly that the reason he didn't say much was because he couldn't make it up. The fiasco with his fake name (was he Mike or Mark?) told you that he couldn't remember the lies he did tell.

He was asked by Andy if he'd always been an archaeologist. I was washing up. Andy was alphabetising his tinned food and Bridget was sniffing the mould on the various half-eaten pots of yoghurt in the fridge. They had been swapping stories about other jobs. Andy had worked in town planning and was single-handedly responsible for some hideous ring road encircling a new town in Hertfordshire. Bridget tried to give everyone a hard-on by talking about the time she'd worked as a stripper doing the rounds of the pubs and clubs of mid and South Wales to pay for her archaeology course at Aberystwyth. Back rooms and bare tits and beer. I told them about digging out a canal basin in Wolverhampton. My story was true.

Then Bridget homes in on Evan/Mike/Mark. Harsfeld. Take your pick.

'What about you Mark? You always done this?'

'I did research,' is all he came up with, 'after my degree.'

'Into what?' Bridget asked. I was laughing. Any idiot could have seen that coming. Bridget was now tipping the dregs out of three different wine bottles into a jug. She stirred it with a wooden spoon as she waited for the answer.

'Post-grad stuff. Nothing exciting.'

Bridget licked her finger, poured herself a glass and offered some to Evan/Harsfeld/Whojit. He declined the offer and was attempting a getaway.

'How boring exactly?' asks Andy, alphabetising his soups by variety, a sub-classification under soups. 'On the Richter scale eh? Bugs and grubs? Nematodes? I've got a mate who studies them for an organics firm. What was it?'

Evan looked anxious at this. Abandoned his mug of tea and the makings of a sandwich. 'Carbon dating.' His words reached us after his body had physically exited the space. Andy and Bridget instantly forgot him. I considered here was a man who did not want to visit his past.

I was wicked. In the hall leading to the bathroom I bumped into him. Not entirely accidental. When any one of us needed to hide the showers/toilets were the only privacy.

'Which university Mark?' all friendly, hail-fellow. I watched him bristle and squirm.

'Edinburgh,' he said suddenly, like a gasp. Then he locked himself in shower room three.

I finished in the bathroom, using the disabled loo because it was more private. The others had doors that were too short somehow, you were visible from the knees down. As I headed back to my room I was thinking about the Roman latrines we had been uncovering. Communal. With a sponge on a stick for wiping your backside. As I turned I noticed that on the noticeboard was a leaflet. A Royal Day Out in Edinburgh.

After that I tuned in hard. No mention of parents. No mention of any relationships. No names to connect to his own. He managed one evening to tell us about some doomed fling involving an older divorced woman and a younger, inexperienced woman and how he'd been torn between the two and that the relationships had been broken off pretty much during his mother's lingering death which he had sort of assisted by upping her morphine dose a couple of evenings.

Bridget was all consoling, gathering him to her bosom and stroking his hair. For once he did not pull away. Andy wanted to know if the two women had ever met, and was actually fishing for a threesome. Evan/Mike/Mark escaped into Bridget's bosom. Hell of a hiding place.

I sat and considered that perhaps Evan/Mike/Mark's real name might be Paul Morel or simply David Herbert Lawrence. I reflected how few books people have read.

He told them he'd been travelling. Been out of the country for some years. Had been 'researching' at Carnac in France.

Carnac my eye. He had been a vagrant, a tramp, it had been written all over him when he first arrived. He was hiding. He was lying. He was afraid. And this was the thing, he was afraid of himself. You only had to watch him twitch, to stare at his shadow as if it was following him, to know the truth. Evan Bees had been to Hell, not Europe.

It rained for about two weeks. When it wasn't raining hard it was an intensive drizzling. We erected plastic tenting over the dig areas to try and limit the mud. Mud has no limits. It is a wild, sucking thing.

I was sheltering under the tenting with Evan/Whojit/D. H. Lawrence. I'd brought tea and no conversation. We were getting on well because I didn't make small talk. I participated if he started up but I didn't initiate. Not since 'Edinburgh' at any rate. You might say I was sly. After all, I was the one person who genuinely listened, who took in information. Whatever you told me I would sift and hold and catalogue.

'I bloody hate rain,' his voice crackled under the plastic shelter. He looked out. 'At home, I used to shut myself in the dining room and turn some music on. Bloody depressing sound if you ask me.'

I registered 'at home'. He'd had one, then.

'Was a tip that room. Full of junk. Neither of us ever even ate in that room. She put a table in the kitchen. Like her mother.' He finished with an odd little snort. Drained the tea mug, tipped the contents onto a mudpatch spattered with drowning blades of grass and turned back to the trench.

At home. Us. I wondered if this Us was Annie. Or if Annie had split up Us. That was why he was here. See how the possibilities start to open up?

He never said he wasn't married. Come the moment when Bridget, tired of his unresponsiveness asked, 'Are you married Mark?' Evan/Mark shook his head. His eyes couldn't keep contact with Bridget.

'Divorced then?'

He looked pained. Couldn't confirm or deny. Not even with a shake of his head. Bridget, wishing to find something wrong with him that wouldn't make her unattractive, latched onto the idea of a painful divorce. Aversion therapy that would make any man think twice about getting involved on any level with another woman. Not me speaking. That's what I overheard her discussing with Andy in the kitchen later. After this she adopted gentler tactics. Sitting near. Brushing against. A hint or glance. All coy.

She let her hair down one evening. Her usual style was an untidy bun pinned or speared by a variety of hair accessories, most of them with broken edges, worn-off gold paint. It was always tumbledown, home dyed, at least three different shades of brown.

This particular evening she had redyed it one solid colour, a burnished red. Thing is, she had no idea how beautiful she looked. Washed. Hair brushed, swept to the front of one shoulder. Her saggy moth-eaten bathrobe. Her bare feet. Eating yoghurt out of the pot with a soup spoon. Reading a magazine on the work top. Bridget not trying. The Real Bridget. No one saw her that night except me. They had gone to the pub. It was like glimpsing a kingfisher as you cycle down the towpath. An electrical blue flash, fleeting and rare.

I savoured the moment and no more. I wasn't about to embark on a sexual liaison with Bridget. Bridget would be staying around and that would lead to all manner of unfinished business. That's my pragmatic view. If you poke my romantic side I might tell you that I was already unconsciously under Annie's spell. Or at least, the spell the gods were casting for us.

They rolled in quite late and Evan/Mike/What's-my-name decided to steal some bread for toast. Clearly the art of foraging is a hard thing to kick out of. Evan Bees was adept at filching foodstuffs, had had years of training. Like Snow White he would take a little from this bowl, a slice from that loaf, a biscuit from that packet, a splash of milk from this jug. Slivers and sips. If you steal a handful of teabags you get caught. If you steal one a day, in turn, from everyone, you never have to buy tea. It's the boiling frog idea.

Evan chose his moment well. Andy was in the showers. Bridget had gone to bed hours ago. As the only woman she was privileged to have a room to herself. Her privacy was only intruded upon once or twice by the odd female hiker. There were two freckled girls from New Zealand one week. Even I kept clear of them. They spoke in code, their own language to shut out others. One morning I found Bridget asleep in one of the airport lounge chairs by the fire doors in the corridor.

So. Everyone's busy or asleep. I wasn't in the kitchen. I was standing by the airport lounge chairs near the fire doors in the corridor, which is partly why I was remembering the New Zealanders. I was looking out across the overgrown courtyard formed by the layout of the buildings. There were wild buddleia there. In the daytime the huge purple flowers scented the air with butter and honey. Whenever the sun managed to shine down into that courtyard there were so many butterflies drinking the nectar that it looked as if the bushes were growing them. Peacock and painted lady blooms, flittering.

I'm gazing into the emptied night, remembering this spectacle of nature, when I see movement in the kitchen. There is a long row of windows above the sinks. I see Evan. I see the theft. A couple of slices of Bridget's bread. Some of Andy's cheese. As he stood by the toaster waiting for his booty to be done he caught sight of me. There was a long moment and then I gave him a sort of salute. A sign of acknowledgment.

By the time I had got round to the kitchen Evan/Mark/Mike was eating the evidence. He looked guilty and all I did was brew some tea.

Everyone was in bed. The hostel was locked up for the night and I was enjoying the solitude of the common room, the comfy chair. A hand of clock patience on the wooden coffee table. Evan Bees took a glass of milk (property of?), a flick through a magazine and a couple of coughs before he approached me. He simulated interest in the game, making small understated astonished or cheering noises. As I picked up the cards and began to shuffle he made his play.

'How did you lose your eye?'

Floored me. I'd expected some ingratiating comment. Some sort of you-scratch-my-back deal he might broker. Instead he'd gone for a vulnerability. My view is he thought he intended to be sympathetic and win me over. That's when I'm feeling charitable. In reality he hoped to find a weak spot. Something to hold against his thievery. An eye for an eye, as they say.

He perched on the arm of the chair opposite. He shocked me because he was the only person ever to ask outright. I had noted Bridget's stolen glances at my eye patch but she'd never asked. Andy had had a good long nosey at it the first day, addressing all his chit-chat to it, staring, memorising. Then onwards, not bothered. Others had a quick embarrassed glance and then studiously addressed their look to my right eye.

Evan Bees, fair play, asked a forthright question.

'I understand if it is too traumatic to recall.'

I smiled to myself.

'I'll tell you how I lost the eye…' I said, leaning to deal a hand of klondike. Seven on seven. '…if you tell me about Annie.'

Moments later I was once again enjoying the solitude of the empty common room.

That night Andy is with Bridget and Evan Bees sleeps once more under the bunk. He has spent most of the time hidden in the shower room but when he thinks I am asleep he skulks in. I listen to him in the dark as he packs his bag and I'm panicking that I won't ever know. He settles at last and I am willing him to sleep. He falls eventually and although it is fitful, he begins to talk and the pieces that are Annie come spilling out of him. I don't have all the corners yet, but I have some of the middle of this puzzle. As he murmurs and stirs she is there, like a ghost.

Following day. Evan Bees is out before anyone and the rumour is he is having breakfast at the roadside café near the fort. Or the town, as it is fast becoming. We all head out later. We find him in the new edge of settlement trench looking for the perimeter walls of what we thought was a villa. He's already knee-deep in a hoard of amber beads.

Doesn't look up. Keeps digging. It's as if all the history of the site is rushing towards him, showing itself, revealing its secrets. Turns up more beads. A knife blade with an ornate and virtually intact hilt. Bronze. Decorated. A fragment of the leather sheath that held it. A handle from a bronze bucket. The hilt of a broadsword. Variety of ornate and perfectly preserved bone combs.

Bone.

He hits the first pelvis at about eleven. He goes easy and, with concerted brushing and an abandonment of both eleven o'clock tea break and one-thirty lunch break, he uncovers the whole pelvis and is starting to reveal femurs. He calls in two of the archaeology students that are on attachment this month and they all brush and chip and dig.

Ribs. Scapula. Sternum crushed in on the vertebrae below and behind. Humerus. Fibula. Tibia. Latin terms. Would our buried pelvises have understood them?

As the students uncover hands, Evan hits the motherlode and finds two skulls. One belongs to this body, the other has rolled in from another burial. As earth is moved so the other skeletons appear. By half past four Evan and his students have partially uncovered the confirmed remains of one woman and three other skeletons, yet to be confirmed as male or female. The second skull appears to be male but the bones remaining have not yet given up their secret identities.

Above us. Hot July. Thunderhead massing. A mob of livid grey-purple nimbus clouds are piling and tumbling, blotting out the daylight. The air is a surreal mix of heavy pressure and cool temperature. Bridget develops a headache. One of the students leaps suddenly from the skeleton dig as he starts a nosebleed. He is helped to the portakabin where the computer is set up, and the first-aid kit. Bridget goes with him to find an aspirin.

Evan Bees never looks up into any of the faces of those around the trench. I am a short distance away finishing for the day on the granary floor we're uncovering. I'm erecting a rain shelter and the wind rattles it from time to time, assessing it. Will it be back later to blow it down? It rattles on through the site, not bothering. There is an audible gasp of excitement as two more skulls, or at least the bottom jaw of one and the eye socket of another, emerge from the dirt.

Bridget Flinch is in deep discussion with a beardy bloke from the National Trust who commutes every day to have a nosey round. They are without a doubt the highest points on that land.

It is Evan Bees who is struck by lightning.

Struck

THEY THOUGHT he might have been struck by lightning.

We had been battered by electrical storms. The town was alive with the sound of fire engines responding to strikes. Blazing chimneys, battered rooftops, a fire in the church opposite the library. St Mark's. Shortly after, when it was discovered that the damage was going to run to a million pounds and it would be cheaper to knock down the church and build new, the vicar resigned. He turned in his dog collar and ran away with the lady who was in charge of the flower arranging. She was married.

The local paper ran a story detailing their love affair, comments from friends and relatives all left shocked and winded by the events. The vicar had thought it was the Hand of God. A thunderbolt sent to make him do the right thing. The right thing was to be honest about his love. To be brave. To stand up and be counted. To open a florist shop in the next big town.

They thought the dead man might have been struck by lightning. Marcia had forgotten to put the bin out and was sneaking out, picking her way in her slippers through the puddles. It was half five in the morning. She tripped over him.

He was lying on the top step of a set of three stone steps that move you up towards her handkerchief lawn. He was wet. Had been lying there some time. He looked as if he had been sunbathing or was relaxing after a tiring swim. Except for his wide-open eyes. Marcia's neighbour, Alan, had been heading home after his late shift. He had already done the right thing and called the police.

In the yard Police Constable Terry Adam was looking over the body and calling for an ambulance and all the legal stuff. He'd made a decision. This young man had been hit by lightning as he cut through the gardens on his way home. It was all very simple to a police mind. It was about calm talk on a two-way radio. It was about uniformed efficiency, a friendly smile. He draped a bench cover over the body and asked Marcia if she'd like to make a cup of tea while they waited for the ambulance. He could take down a statement.

Faced with this, Marcia didn't think twice apparently. She just turned to her son, Justin, who was yawning in the back doorway and said, 'Get Annie.'

Justin was surprised that I answered the basement door without him knocking. If truth be told I think I freaked him out. It was early enough in the morning for him to think that I was still asleep probably, and dreaming probably. He didn't know that I'd had a wakeful night, going over Fran Dart's details trying to work out ways of looking for her. I had seen him coming down the steps.

I think everyone was wakeful that morning. The air was clearer now after the storm. The noises and the freshness combined to

keep everyone awake and if the weather heated up in the afternoon they would all be asleep at their desks or at the wheels of
their buses, in front of their classes. The fire at St Mark's was
raging still, sending its own nimbus clouds of thick black smoke
heavenwards.

At Marcia's I didn't go through the house. I squeezed through
the side gate. The house rises tall against the side of a banking
and her little side entrance is narrow, stonework on the house
side and a damp banking of grass and wildflowers on the other.
It rises above your head, mosses and ferns encroach on the stone
path. Through the gate at the end. Only this time I didn't get to
the gate. He was blocking the way. The young man was wearing
a chocolate brown T-shirt and chocolate brown jeans. He looked
surprised.

'I don't get it,' he said, although it was clear from the wavering,
teary tone of his voice that he did get it and it was sinking in.
Sure as mud.

'I don't get this. Where am I?'

'You're in Marcia's garden,' I said, trying to keep it calm and
friendly. 'The end house on Archbold Terrace. Do you know
where that is?'

'Yeah. Yeah, I was cutting down the back lane. Heading home.'

He looked hemmed in now. Didn't look back. Marcia had a
lot of trouble with the right of way, the back lane, that ran the
length of the terrace. Her insurance premiums were upped
annually on the strength of that access path. It was hidden and
it was easy to get in at the back of any of the houses and not be
seen, either from the road or from the other houses. It backed
onto a dense woodland. It was pretty in the daytime and sinister
at night, as if wolves or witches might come out of there.

He wasn't looking back, because he could have seen his dead
self. I didn't push this.

'You were heading home. From the pub?'

'He's so fucking jealous…Christ…'

'What's your name?'

I could almost hear the crumpling of a form. I was getting very efficient.

'I wanted to. He knows that. But I never.'

'Can you remember what happened?'

He was shaking his head, teary-eyed, his throat making odd gaspy, raspy noises as he struggled with tears. You'd think he was crying because he was dead. You'd be wrong. He was crying because he knew who had killed him. Aunt Mag would have described him as 'beside himself'. In more ways than one.

'I never. I never. I wanted to, but I never. He's so fucking jealous…I never. I wanted, but I never.'

He sobbed it out. Then he walked past me, through me and disappeared into the darkness at the front of the house. The streetlights were out tonight. The storm.

'Who were you talking to?' said a voice. I spun round. It was Terry Adam, giving me a hard stare. He glanced over my shoulder, as if I might be hiding someone. A suspect. He didn't speak. He seemed to be off in a trance for an instant and then he rubbed his hand across his face, looked very tired suddenly, took in a breath.

'What are you doing here?'

I had stalked Oliver Howard for a week. Now here I was spectating at a mystery death. Marcia was there to save me from the Inquisition.

'She's a friend. I called her over. Feeling a bit dodgy myself.'

Terry Adam looked blank. Yes. That is it, as if he was blanking it out. The words came out of his mouth by rote.

'Be prepared for some delayed reaction.'

He flicked open his notebook. Clicked his pen a few times. It was only afterwards that I realised he was standing in the alley so that he too could avoid looking at the green bench cover and thinking about who was underneath it. He was attentive and businesslike. Taking notes. Then he opted to take a short hike back along the lane. As he disappeared into the early dawning light, his Maglite torch a shooting star, Marcia leaned towards me.

'Did you get to speak to him?'

She nodded her head towards the body, sprawled under the bench cover.

'Not really. Just confusion. Jealousy. And he's gone, in case you're worried.'

'Well, always worth a try eh? And if he comes back I can give you a bell.' Marcia, ever the pragmatist.

Terry Adam was moving back across the handkerchief lawn now and I shut up. Could not help looking, frankly, shifty. Marcia glugged at her tea, poured the dregs onto some ropey-looking nasturtiums in the nearest flowerbed and said she'd better get in and get dressed.

We stood there a moment. He managed a smile. It was painful to see, his policeman politeness-training smile. It was a smile he had practised in front of a mirror. Passed exams in. A smile he had copied from a series of instructional smiling photographs in a training manual. And now his face was shifting into a neutral look as we heard the ambulance arrive and Justin came running through the house.

'They're here.'

Marcia trotted inside. Terry Adam looked right at me then, for just a nanosecond. If I hadn't turned I would have missed it. But I did turn. His eyes locked mine. It was like one of those shooting star moments when you happen to glance at the night and a star scorches the sky above you. Something rare. Something electric. Before he looked away.

The ambulance team arrived and we were separated suddenly by a gurney clattering, by fluorescent jackets and quick efficiency. Without looking my way again, Terry Adam accompanied the body as the young man, Danny, was bagged up and wheeled away as swiftly as a dog turd in the park.

Next morning it was clear that Danny had put the word out in Heaven. I was a useful police informant in the 'missing presumed dead' department.

Hence the presence of a dog at breakfast. A little chocolate brown terrier skittered into the kitchen as I yawned over the kettle. The elderly lady followed after him, in her chocolate brown cagoule and sensible outfit. Her glasses had a lens broken.

'I'm not in Keswick,' she said as she clipped the chocolate brown lead onto the dog and I fetched my coat to put on over my pyjamas.

At the police station, I realised I had made two mistakes. Pyjamas and police station. I did not make a third, I turned around and headed homewards, where I read in the morning paper that Mrs Bannister was missing and had turned up before in a b & b in Keswick. She had said very clearly that this was where she was not, and I was so frustrated I could have screamed.

Instead, I found myself back at the police station, still in my pyjamas, only this time I was glad to see that the desk staff seemed to have abandoned their post. Instead, Sergeant Laidlaw came to my aid.

'Can I help you?' he asked. I had to be careful, because I could see the CCTV monitor noseying at me. I made certain I had my back to the camera and that I looked as if I was terribly interested in the *Crime: Together We'll Crack It* leaflets on the desk.

The camera would not pick up Sergeant Laidlaw. And I told him straight that Mrs Bannister was not in Keswick. Indeed, Mrs Bannister herself turned up with her little dog, who Sergeant Laidlaw was very taken with and chucked under the chin, and told him straight too. 'I'm not in Keswick.'

'Leave it with me,' said Laidlaw and took custody of Mrs Bannister. I left the police station. Hopeful. Helpful.

Later that week the evening paper declared that Mrs Bannister was found on a ledge at Long Way Crop. A scar in the stonework showed where she lost her footing and a scree bank gave way beneath her stumbling feet. Sliding her, slithering her down to land heavily on the outcrop, cracking her skull on a jutting piece of the crags. Her glasses were splintered. A small piece of flesh and hair identified the rock that killed her. Her dog was strangled by the leash, caught round her wrist like a snake. A birdwatcher following an owl spotted the dog dangling from the outcrop.

Long Way Crop. Where Evan is captured in time. His face, in that moment, looking out at the view. Beyond me.

The Jims

IDECIDED TO catch up with the Jims. I had never yet attended a meeting at the Spiritualist Church where there were not one or two stray Jims knocking about. And yet if you check the data for years gone by you will struggle to find Jim as a top-ranking name. It is not there amongst the Timothys and the Daniels, the Johns and the Davids. Lazarus has ranked higher. Although I suppose since James is up there that's probably how it happens. Even in the fifties, despite *Lucky Jim*, it didn't enjoy a surge of popularity. But, it remains, there is a stack of Jims in the airspace above Heaven.

At the LookOut I started straight away with a catalogue constructed entirely for the Jims. Word got out telepathically quickly. My brainwave washed up in the Waiting Room of Heaven and presented me with five men and two women. All called Jim.

There is Jim Brewer who was always known as Jim but whose

real name was Gerald. His misnomer began with what he described as 'a bright spark in the clerks' department' who had a habit of giving everyone a nickname. Until the Bright Spark's arrival Gerald had always been Gerald or, more formally, Mr Brewer. The young clerk arrived and for inexplicable reasons started to refer to Gerald, Mr Brewer, as Jim. He was politely corrected on several hundred occasions but continued with the Jim.

Finally, one overheated July afternoon when Mr Brewer had discovered that his wife had been carrying on with Lionel from the golf club and was discomfited by the runnels of sweat trickling down his back and in streams and rivulets from his armpits he exploded at the Bright Spark. Why did he persist with this Jim business?

The Bright Spark's comment was that he looked like a Jim. Gerald Brewer raised his voice in the office. Raised it enough for people to look up from pencil sharpenings and account books.

And it was all utterly bloody pointless because the Bright Spark still called him Jim. Just as he persisted in calling Muriel on the switchboard Gloria.

When I asked Gerald/Jim what the Bright Spark's name was he said that was the problem. He couldn't remember. All he could remember was that when the Bright Spark had got himself a new job, a promotion, Gerald had signed the leaving card 'Best wishes, Jim'.

Gerald's wife left him and a new woman arrived in the department. Vanessa. She shook his hand with a firm grip and smelt of vanilla and freesia. She was formal and polite and addressed him as Mr Brewer. Before he knew what he was saying he was smiling and informing her, 'Everyone calls me Jim.'

Jim. Jim. Under the crisp clean bedsheets of their first Friday night together. And he felt like a new man, casting off the husk that had been Gerald Brewer to become Jim and Vanessa.

There was Jim/James Crowthorne who was looking for his estranged twin brother Jonathon and having no luck. There was Jim Tennant and his motorcycle accident. Jim Match worrying about his accounts and the trouble he had caused his widow that he wanted to set right. Cousin Jim and his whisky chasers.

Of the two women, one had spent her youth disguised as Jim and travelled out of Liverpool on the big steamers to America and Australia. The other had always been known as Jim because she hated the name Jemima.

Part of the problem with the Spiritualist Church at Hackett Lane was Alan Carney. Because basically he couldn't hear or see any chocolate-brown-clad people he caused problems. Standing on the platform trying to use 'Jim' as a starting point is all very well unless you happen to be one of the Jims. I remembered Jim the butcher and Jim the security guard that night I had met Sidney Colville. I remembered how I had sorted things out. I had stepped up to the platform and made myself useful. To promise messages and not deliver them was frustrating. It began unfinished business, all the Jims loitering in perpetuity.

This became my mission for the month. November. Heading inevitably towards December. Business at the LookOut was quite slow that month, not because people were not vanishing on a daily basis, popping out for a newspaper and being found, months later, lapdancing in Tenerife. No.

Chiefly because Terry Adam had stopped sending them on to me. He did not believe I was a medium. He had his flag planted firmly in the Sam Cartwright camp. I was mentally ill and shouldn't be encouraged. All this talk of being a medium was simply my cry for help, or whatever the current psychobabble term for it was.

There was a clock on it, an alarm that would go off on the

fifth of December when Evan Bees' legally-dead paperwork was stamped and made official. Stamped with a huge skull and cross-bones. Solicitors would exchange brown manila files and cash cheques for services rendered. Possibly there would be a fanfare of bugles playing the Last Post in the town square and somewhere a flag would fly at half mast.

More likely Evan Bees would have his file consigned to the oblivion of some public records office. He'd be catalogued at the back of some grey tin filing cabinet and later transferred to microfiche.

I wanted a flaming arrow to be shot from the park. Set light to a rowing boat on the lake at Goatmill, cut it adrift to sputter and burn.

Whatever might mark the day, it was the day I was scheduled to 'get over it, get on with life, get a job, get a house'. Stop this nonsense. See sense.

It made me edgy. I had my reality, however different it might be from the reality of others. This underworld was where I lived. I had come to terms with it. Sort of. It was the 'sort of' that threw me. I knew I couldn't not do this. It would be like making a left-handed person write with their right hand. I could see that. I could feel what wasn't right. I was here. Living inside my head. With my demons.

Is that what they are? I have spent time thinking back over the people who've spoken to me. I've gone over and over the conversations and the messages, the anxieties. I've filtered and sifted and searched. They seem ordinary enough. Even Hal and the Fisherman's wife. They weren't evil. They did not intend harm. They were just more intense. As if in dying, in letting go, they let go of more than simply breathing, beating their hearts. For them, everything was brought up short, there is no longer time for good manners. There's just now to get it done.

I sat in my old spoonback saloon chair in the basement. I watched the housemaid come down the stairs and hang up her shabby, thin, chocolate brown coat and make her way through the bricked-up door to the scullery. I could hear her now start to sing.

She sang every day, despite being late, despite her inadequate coat and the cold November weather. She sang 'Tea for Two' and 'Your Feet's Too Big'. I listened. I realised that what I had was an added extra.

I tried to find her in the electoral records for the house. It was cold in the library, Lara was in a cocoon of homeknit jumpers because the boiler was on the fritz again. I scoured all the records with Lara. We looked up when 'Tea for Two' and 'Your Feet's Too Big' were written and recorded and used that as our start date. But I'd forgotten that she wasn't old enough to be included. Women's suffrage began with the over thirties and clearly she was not eighteen yet. For sixty years she had been not eighteen yet.

She worked for the Rothwells. Mr Henry Rothwell and his wife Ginny who owned all of this house and another, more country-mansion-style house, near the coast. If you want to you can trace their history in the local archives. Big Wig. Bigger Cheese. Top Dog. The Rothwells cut a dash through our small town society. There are sepia tinted photographs in the drawers showing their wedding, where Mrs Rothwell looks as if a net curtain has fallen on her head as she was leaving the house.

It was a good marriage for Henry Rothwell. He had money, self-made timber merchant. She had no money but impeccable table manners and that priceless commodity—class.

Open-top cars, garden parties, tennis trophies. They took up where the Whitworths left off. But these photographs tell you nothing about their inner life. And this little housemaid is forgotten. She isn't anywhere in any archive. Yet I suppose the Rothwells couldn't function without her. I don't see Ginny Rothwell as the kind of woman who would polish her own silverware or iron her own chemise.

I had never spoken with her. I confess that as she came and went I'd been a little afraid of her, of what she might tell me, the things I would have to share with her. Then I thought: I have no one to share anything with, and that is what I need. Maybe that is what she needs. Someone. Me. Customer Service. Translator. Messenger Girl. She won't think I'm a freak. She will think I am a connection.

I was very careful not to frighten her. She was wedged carefully into her routine. Indeed as I spoke up she looked anxious. Here was someone who was going to make her even later.

'If you're after Mrs Rothwell you'll need to go to the front door. Down here you'll just get Mrs Willis, the housekeeper.' She was pushing through the brick, into the scullery.

'What's your name?' I asked, reaching out to touch her arm, not thinking that my arm would go straight through hers. She did not notice. She did not realise that she was even later than she thought. The Late Housemaid.

Another voice then, in the distance, yelled for her. 'Florrie? You late again?' and she pushed on through the wall. On her way into the blackness that had once been a scullery.

I sat back in the chair, stayed there until it grew dark.

I think Jim Night became a part of clearing my decks, moving forward.

I decided that I would hire the Whitworth Plain Speaking Hall for one evening. I would advertise the event and in the same way that people came to the Spiritualist Church so they would be able to turn up here and we could take a crack at the Jims.

I felt a little guilty since the seven Jims who had been sitting in the Waiting Room watching Mrs Berry crochet antimacassars had been getting along famously. They played cards, talking long into the night about their lives and loves. They were relaxed and at ease. And yet I wanted rid of them. They needed to be elsewhere. They needed to move on.

I called in at the Whitworth Plain Speaking Hall to enquire about prices and availability. The hall has two tiers, stalls and a circle all in a tight horseshoe, anyone sitting in the circle can just about lean down and touch the people on the stage. At the back are rows of wooden chairs with racks in the back for hymn sheets and music. There are the ranked and decorated pipes for the pipe organ which is being restored.

The hall used to be always busy with church choirs and religious meetings, beetle drives and, of course, plain speaking. It had gone through a decline and some dry rot but when the local councillor and architect, Brett Andrews, put forward the motion of demolishing it to build our very own Millennium Hall there was nearly a riot. Funds flooded in to restore the place, a local timber merchant (no longer a Rothwell) provided the joists and rafters that were needed free of charge and then threw in the materials for the restoration of the oak panelling. All sorts of events were planned and the Whitworth Plain Speaking Hall is really busy again. Strippers, gospel choirs, opera nights. Jim Night.

Brett Andrews has a firm of architects in town. He's responsible for a lot of new building projects in the area, county-wide, not just in town. His ideas are very futuristic involving lots of glass and suspension cables. The out-of-town retail park where Sam's dealership is was revamped by Brett Andrews' company recently. There is new office space, it is like a group of jellyfish around a Japanese garden. No one has yet rented the office space.

When it is dark in town by mid-afternoon and the wintry lights flick on in the shops and the hideous concrete sixties office blocks, I like to walk out to the retail park and see the winter light through Brett Andrews' buildings. It is a longer day by those office spaces. Then I walk up to the Crags, as I did all those years ago with My Mother, and the Brett Andrews jellyfish buildings begin to glimmer, transforming it into an ocean dotted and spangled with streetlights and the scudding flashes of headlights. It feels like my place up there on the hillside with the darkness and the stars.

I advertised carefully. I used posters and placed adverts in the paper, for town and also the next town and a couple of the out-lying villages. I had an odd plan, really. I wanted to do this and yet I didn't want to draw undue attention to the event. I didn't want a circus. It wasn't intended to be a show. I was wearing my customer service hat again.

Jim Night was my way of putting myself back on track. Few people had understood. Most people were scared of me or considered me a freak; even, I believed, My own Mother. Now I realised that I didn't care what they thought. Get on with it. Remember?

Marcia was good enough to provide refreshments with help from Atalanta and some of her Glade girls. As I had thought, she was a custodian, keeping up My Mother's tradition of rescu-ing girls and giving them the space to find out that they were heading the wrong way, but it wasn't too late to check out the map and change direction.

One of her most recent protégées was Aileen. Whilst at The Glade at Goatmill Aileen had discovered a hidden talent for carpentry and was now enrolled in a course at the college studying cabinetmaking. Atalanta was convinced Aileen was going to be the next Chippendale. Lara was there too with her notebook computer ready to take down any details that might need to be researched. We were going all out for the Jims.

We prepared for the evening, small notebooks and pencils on each seat for things that people might want to write down rather than say. Marcia was at the back of the hall opening the wooden hatch to the kitchen; inside the urn was starting to steam and there was the comforting cluckle of cups and saucers being set out. Vanilla and almond aromas mingled with a century of floor polish and Pledge as Atalanta unloaded trays of buns and cakes, cut into slabs of fruit loaf. It snowed icing sugar.

Lara was at the side of the stage setting up her database with a log book people could sign if they were alive, and another log book for the Dead who checked in.

It occurred to me that I had friends. Real friends who cared enough to do this. People who accepted me and my open frequency.

There was a flashing moment. Golden. Trumpets. Golden trumpets even. And I considered that what I needed was love. I had fear and anger, sorrow, grief, confusion. If I could just have love, it would complete the set.

Into this crept hope. There's another one. Pauline Dart had bags of that she carried around. It staved off grief and shored up her love.

I don't think there is happiness. I think that is something cheap and plastic that they sell from cereal boxes. I think the real McCoy is made from pieces of all the other items, the grief, the fear, the anger. There are moments, possibly months at a time, when everything we are fuses and we are there. We are real and it is so much we haven't the words for it. Certainly not happiness. You can't bottle this.

I was catching philosophy.

Yeah. Right. Wait around for the cure. See, I'd caught cynicism too.

The Jims, my seven plus many others, began to arrive, filtering through the walls, down from the ceiling, up through the platform, moving first into the periphery of my vision and then into focus. I began to take notes with Lara's help, relaying the messages to her, and we were engaged in doing this as Marcia and Atalanta let in the crowd. Lara's hands were shaking and she smiled up at me once.

The seats filled. I filled with apprehension. The sight of the relatives they had come to see started a ripple of anxiety amongst the Jims. They started to shove forward at me now, all talking at once in a tense, excited gabble. It mixed with the humming chat from the crowd and I felt a sudden surge of panic.

It was a free event. I wondered how many people had come here to laugh or to make trouble. How many to shelter from the rain. I told the Jims, one at a time please. I asked them in a calm voice and they reacted. They calmed, and the first Jim pointed out his daughter, at the back.

'Tell her, Shortbread, there she is... The tall one in the blue shirt. Tell her if he hasn't asked by now, he's never bloody going to.'

I stood on the platform, no music, no introduction and I pointed at the tall woman in the blue shirt.

'Excuse me... Shortbread?'

She reacted, stiffened visibly and stayed with her back half to me. I realised that it was quite hard to be the first, to have attention drawn to you this way. It didn't improve with the message.

'Your dad, Jim, says, if he hasn't asked you to marry him by now, he's never bloody going to.'

There was a ripple of reaction. Not from her. She stood as if frozen in time, half turned. Utterly motionless. The ripple ran through the crowd. The next Jim came forward. He was looking over the audience anxiously, checking for his loved one. His messagee.

'Can't spot her. Can't see her, Annie…'

'Never mind, just give me the message.'

'Buckets and spades. She'll know.'

So I called out the message and up in the circle two teenage girls started to squeal with reaction and delight before making their way along the row and hurrying up the back stairs. Still squealing.

And that is how it ran. I spoke directly to people. I used names, pet names, picked them out like suspects in an identity parade. Those who thought they would give nothing away in case they were spotted and used didn't have to give anything away. I told them what the message was, and I moved on. No audience manipulation. No reading body language. I got on with the job in hand.

The Whisky Chasers Cousin Jim had been so fond of turned out to be a group of his mates, all equally fond of Scotch. Or Irish. Quality and Quantity had been their motto. They came to the front all dressed in black suits but each wearing a colourful tie. There was a toast, and a glass of whisky was set alight on the edge of the platform. It burned with a blue and pink flame.

A couple of audience members got up to leave then, shuffling their way sideways along the seating, people who hadn't got their message. People leaving empty handed, heavy hearted. If you were expecting poetry or wisdom you'd be disappointed. There was no Crown Derby china on Jim Night, either. Small messages of love and goodbye, the things left unsaid. The unfinished business from over forty different Jims. Reassurance and letting go. Everyday. Ordinary.

Some of the Jims also went away empty handed. Jims whose

loved ones had not shown up, who were probably dead, the Jims had been hanging around so long. At the end of the evening Lara printed the messages I had relayed, the ones that hadn't found a listener.

It was Lara who commented it was like a lonely hearts. Missing Jim seeks widow Laura with news of shed keys. Not that there had been any shed keys this evening. Apart from Jim Match finally settling his ledgers with his wife and accountant, all the treasure map/hidden Vermeer/Crown Derby coffee pot messages had been at a minimum.

But Lara's comment made me think and I decided to print the messages in the small ads of the local newspapers, maybe in a couple of the nationals too. Just a small ad, to whom it may concern. In the mystery and puzzle of answers there would be enlightenment for someone. In buckets and spades.

Jim Night had been quiet but successful. I felt rested somehow, like ticking off an item on a list. I had been, at last, a translator. Customer service representative. I had got the job done. I thought that this night I would sleep really well for the first time in an age. I was relaxed and certain. Atalanta dropped me off at the LookOut basement. I waved as I got the keys out and opened the door.

The woman came right through me with a shudder then, and was gone. I waited. Not sure it was her. Not wanting it to be her. Someone I had never met, and yet so familiar. Moments later she was back, stepping through me again. This time I was certain. This time I stepped with her. Heading out into the darkness.

I stepped out into the basement yard, shut the door behind me and started walking.

Dig Deep with Arthur:
eye for an eye

He had one eye bandaged and a bald patch just above it. The eye was safe but the bald patch would most likely never regrow. The burn extended down his left side and he had some nerve damage in his left hand that they weren't certain would come right. There was a physiotherapist, Angie, who was very keen and enthusiastic and got his hopes up.

Well. No. Actually, she got her hopes up and projected them onto Evan. Evan had given up all hope by the looks of him. He'd been unconscious for three days. Clearly while he'd been away something had had a word with him. He lay in bed looking out of the window with his right eye, not doing anything much except heal.

I sat with him for over an hour one afternoon. Bridget had been in earlier with a vast bunch of flowers. Evan lay with his all-seeing eye turned away from them. Andy had trawled into town for a box of chocolates, setting down a huge pick-and-mix selection of luxury chocolates from Thorntons. He'd stayed an hour and eaten most of them, leaving Evan a gold box with crumples of gold foil and torn paper ribbons. Now, as I sat by the window so Evan would have to see me I could smell the leftover chocolates, bitter and sweet and sickly.

I was quite happy to sit there although I wasn't allowed a smoke. I had a passing thought about my one-eyed status, but I guessed that me sitting there with my eye patch might make Evan sit up and realise he'd been lucky. His patch would come off and his eye would blink into the sunshine.

I had been allowed cards and I dealt out a hand of klondike. Evan's eye watched the cards. Black on red. Red on black. Shuffle, deal. The riffle and clack of the cards was soothing. Well, was to me. The visiting hours had a few moments to go. I had been told to pack up the cards by the bossy ward sister when suddenly he came out with it.

'My name is Evan Bees.'

His one eye swivelled round to look at me. I nodded, pocketed my cards.

He began. He didn't say, 'Once upon a time', but that's how it turned out.

He told me the Gothic romance of picking over ancient bones with Annie Colville. He spoke of the whiteness of her coat, the sonorous bell sounds the sink made as she washed up the petrie dishes and beakers. How love had set a snare for him in Annie's face.

Then a nurse in a uniform two sizes too small came in, all set to change Evan's bandages, and I was cast out.

As I left, his one eye watched me.

Next afternoon I volunteered for hospital visiting again. No one argued. Andy asked when Evan, or Mark as he knew him, was due out and I pleaded genuine ignorance.

This time Evan was sitting up, legs over the side of the bed, T-shirt and track pants on. He was edgy, picking at a plate of sandwiches. As I stood in the doorway he didn't see me, turned his bandaged eye. Then he turned to pick up his juice drink and spilled it, startled by my presence. Don't misunderstand. He wasn't freaked out by me. He was nervous of what he might reveal. He had a lot of beans to spill.

I handed him some paper towels to mop up the juice. I took them from him when they were used up and binned them. As I looked into the bin I began my own story. A story set in a small backyard in a row of Victorian terraced houses. A yard where my gran grew tomatoes and nasturtiums in chimney pots so that the odd L-shaped space looked like an earthbound roofscape.

Chimney pots, a weather vane that fell off St Thomas' church, old drainpipes standing on end and filled to their swan-neck hoppers with sweet peas and lupins. Tall dark blue delphiniums, as thickly blue as a storm in the sky, spired from the top. Cosmos and bronze fennel spluttered like smoke from crown-topped stacks, mottled and speckled. Ivies of every shape and shade of green poured from the vents and slats of the pots. Scrambled. Clambered. Tangling up with the black-eyed susans and the canary creeper. Empress of India. Alaska mixed. Ipomoea heavenly blue. Some days I thought they looked like castle turrets with their crenellations and cut outs and ledges.

I remember it well. Technicolor. My last view with binocular vision. Do I dream with two eyes? Yes. That's what dreams are for. Take you back. Let you visit.

And there were hens. Three hens and a cockerel in a little run near the coal shed. Not that we had coal by then. Gran kept junk in there mostly, and some of the chicken feed. It was my job to clean out the chickens. I didn't mind it. I got to find the eggs. I kept those hens in a royal manner. Fresh straw. Clean water. I hypnotised them occasionally, drawing a line in the dirt before them.

Tuesday. Never much liked Tuesdays. I was in the coop with my shovel and bucket and the big black rubber gauntlets that my gran gave me to wear. I'd got the hens out into the run, pecking out the corn I'd strewn around. Out of my way. The cockerel had been sitting on the pitched roof.

Then he wasn't. He was ambushing me in the confines of the coop. He is my last memory with my two eyes. A blur of greenish black and gold, the gnarled skin of his feet, the spur at the back of his leg, the claws, yellow, bluish. Feathers and hen shit and blood on the straw.

I banged my head on the rafters of their ceiling trying to get away. He lacerated my arms as I swiped at him, the shovel lost, let go. He was on his territory and he had all the advantages.

Pain. Torch-hot burning and then dizziness and sick rising and stars prickling black in a white-out sky.

It seems like a laugh now. Something so ridiculous it should be videotaped for a TV show. Kid loses an eye to a crazed cockerel. Crazed with sexual jealousy? Who knows. It might be hilarious. A blur of feathers. The comical way I flapped about, crushed in by the coop so I couldn't defend myself. Cooped up as they say.

They patched my face. My arms. There are only slight traces now of the scars that were much angrier when I was a lad. Scars are always angry. They shouldn't be there. Just traces now, his footprints. After I woke up in the hospital I wondered where my eye was. If perhaps Gran had shovelled it away with the straw and muck. If it rolled like a marble at her feet. If it looked like a miniature football with the air let out.

I had a glass eye for a time. Exactly like a marble. So exactly like that I lost it in a game with Andrew Latham. It was highly prized. Everyone wanted to play him for it. He never lost it. And then marble season was over and it was elastics and my eye stayed at home in Andrew Latham's marble bag.

Not much of a view.

I got the eyepatch then. I liked it. I felt at home. Unusual. Different. Settled. There was no point wailing about it. It was done and I had to move on. I ran away from it, put the whole incident behind me. Then I realised that it was not behind me. It was with me all the time. Evidenced by the blank spot under the patch. So that's where it lived. I accommodated it. Concentrated on mastering the art of monocular vision, testing myself, pushing my boundaries. My boundaries expanded.

Gran cleared out the coop and the chicken feed. Bought me a dog who got run over.

After she broke their necks we ate the chickens. Revenge is a dish best eaten cold. With some salad cream and a head of lettuce.

'Revenge,' said Evan Bees. He took in a gasp that might have been choking but was in fact, laughing.

Evan Bees started to laugh. And laugh. And sob.

I waited. Wanting more.

Phone box

IT WAS dark now. Following in Fran Dart's footsteps I had gone beyond the retail park into the maze of the industrial estate. The darkness was blared into at odd points by stark security lights. Great squares of whiteness illuminating yards full of bricks or aggregate, miles of fencing and paving stacked high, sleeping machinery, JCBs with their arms lifted, buckets up as if stretching into a dream. Blank windows. One light left on by mistake in an office. Chain link fences locked with silver padlocks.

One street led into another and back into another and along and round, curving about the whole estate. All roads leading to the Buckingham double glazing and conservatory showroom.

We turned into Haymarket Way, off the Strand, beyond Fenchurch Street, parallel to Regent Street which led into Oxford Street. The double glazing showroom sitting at the head of the Mall. Some council Bright Spark having fun with his

Monopoly board of an industrial centre. Haymarket Way, because it ran off into the fields of the neighbouring farm. Not that it was a farm now. It had been sold off. It was a gravel quarry on one side and a landfill site at the other.

Darkness blotted in as I walked. The rain came on, first great drops slapping into my face, onto my head and as I neared the spiked steel gates of the landfill site it pattered faster and faster like tears. Like sobbing.

Until I saw them. Fran Dart taking up her place amongst four others. Four others, beyond the gate, beckoning Fran back. And then waiting for me as Pauline had waited for her.

They stood for a long moment and looked at me, it was as if they were sorry for me, saying nothing. Giving no clue. Only Fran touched a hand to her neck and I noticed the knotted leather thong, almost like a necklace. But not quite. Too binding. Too biting. They all wore the same.

Then, as if the time was up, they moved back to take up their places, knowing they would not have to wait much longer. Hugging farewell to each other as they moved away. And the world was darkness and water.

Later I remembered being in the phone box, the metallic echo of my voice, the tiny tinny telephone whisper of the police switchboard operator, the smell of urine. Outside the rain battered and still cars were passing, headlights full on sweeping over me like searchlights. I was aware of the disconnection between my sodden clothes and the surface of me, my skin. I was bone cold. I was stone calm.

Walking back, keeping to the grass verges, I was aware of every stitch in my shoes, the muddied earth beneath the wet spikes of grass, the brush of stinging nettles, the earthy waft of dampness from the soaked ground, the ditch. The rattle and shudder of every leaf in the hedgerow. The rhythms of my footsteps. My heart. My breath.

I don't remember town or arriving home. When I awoke I was on the floor still in my drenched clothes. When I looked for my keys they were in the door.

I stayed in. Filling in my ads, checking over Fran Dart's shoebox of belongings looking for a way in. A way out.

I had not seen any newspapers. I didn't take them, didn't want all their true-life trouble and tragedy for fifty pence. I thought of one of the other women, her husband and her children. The thing that I had done. I had taken away their hope and replaced it with grief. I couldn't seem to reconcile this with the agony of waiting.

I thought that as I had waited for Evan so they had waited for her. I thought of the children, to the youngest of whom she would be like someone in a fairytale. A mythical beast like Cinderella or Snow White.

Some back-drawer bit of my brain told me that it was better. It was good. It was moving on, that she and her four companions at the landfill site would be gone now. They'd get to wrestle the angels behind the MDF door. Harp lessons or whatever made you happy. Finished. Done. Have a sit down.

Pauline Dart was waiting for me at the basement when I returned from buying milk. She looked pale and her hair seemed very dark, very shiny and clean. I stood, my heartbeat choking me, waiting for Pauline to turn her head. I could have turned and run, but I didn't. Pauline turned. She looked at me for a long moment and I understood that she would hate me. I understood that she would want her message. What did Fran say? When Fran had said nothing. I had nothing to give her.

I did not understand when she stepped towards me and enfolded me. Her arms wrapping around me, her hair next to my face, smelling of almonds, soft. The strength of her embrace and her voice saying gently, 'Thank you.'

I did not understand why I was crying. Why I sobbed and Pauline soothed me, when it was not my sister they had found in the landfill site.

I couldn't rest in peace. Instead I took out all the items from the shoebox and looked them all over. Searching. What I found, ultimately, what I hadn't admitted I was searching for, were the photocopies of Evan Bees and his cut-out catalogue disguises. He looked out at me, speckled and a bit grainy and I wondered if, at last, I was going to get his message.

December the fifth stood like a wall at the edge of my vision now. I felt as if the race was on. I was going to get there and there'd be the snap of a starting pistol. Would all the chocolate brown crowds be there to cheer me onwards? Evan would be declared dead, which wasn't quite the same as actually being dead. The angels would not get their way. I wondered if they would all be sitting, as I had, eating celestial Bourbon biscuits and waiting for Evan to show his face. I know, he won't ever turn up. Not here. Not there.

The rumours began that the phone box caller on the Goatmill Lake murder and the phone box caller in the Landfill Killer business were the same person. There was an interview on the local radio station with the journalist who wrote the book about the Goatmill case. They were trying to work out how the person is connected, when the murders clearly aren't. DI Knight was interviewed on the radio, most of which had to be bleeped out.

It was the magical mystery of the month, 'Who was the masked avenger?' sort of thing and it was front page because everyone else was behaving. Councillors were concealing their corruption and vices for the moment. No one was riding bareback on wheelie bins on the council estate. I felt guilty even though I hadn't done anything wrong. I was relieved when a cow was run over on the dual carriageway.

Tuesday. I had been in the throes of sorting out the newsletter I had started. Instead of maxing out the classifieds in the local paper, I had brokered a deal with the manager at our local branch of Printshop Special by the station to print up my own small ads in a handy sheet, called, you guessed it, *The LookOut*. He was very helpful, offering his brother's services as a website designer if I fancied going 'webwide' and casting a critical eye over ideas for the banner. I avoided the obvious eyes looking through the double 'O'. Instead I opted for a seafaring chap looking through a telescope.

It was a cheap run of 1,000 copies every Tuesday. I collected them at closing time and distributed them on Wednesday morning. Except at the library. They're closed on Wednesday so I took them straight from Printshop Special and Lara let me into the library to drop them off there. I don't know why I'm telling you all this. Liar that I am. It is to stave off having to tell you that the most important thing that Tuesday morning was Terry Adam.

I did not see his change of clothes at first. What panicked me was that he was inside, going through my belongings, sniffing the mould in a tea mug, picking over my clothes from the back of the chair. Sniffing the underarms like a dog taking scent. I halted in the doorway, feeling like a trespasser in what passed for my home. Then I saw there was something different about his uniform.

He was not in blue. He was dressed in chocolate brown.

'What happened?' I asked. He waved a hand, dismissive.

'Nothing. That's not why I'm here. It's not about that.' He looked at me. He looked so sad that it made me want to look away. The silence that followed was only broken for me by Florrie arriving to hang up her coat. What did Terry want?

What would I have to do? He didn't speak, he just rubbed his face in the same tired way he had in Marcia's side alley.

'Listen. I was out at the landfill the day before…I was just the crowd control…' He started to look around, searching. 'I'm not CID, Annie, so they won't listen to me. But what I saw up there…I think it matters.'

He saw the shoebox then, the trinkets and nicknacks inside. He looked trancelike. Looked as if he had to decide something and he couldn't look at me. Then he took a deep breath. His fingers moved into Fran Dart's shoebox, poking around in her left-behind things. 'Maybe…If I show you…'

Quietly and slowly he took the shoebox items out one by one and arranged them around the central, empty cardboard rectangle of the box. The gold ribbon, the black shell button, the Dutch guilder, the lipstick, the mirror, the paper bag, the toothbrush head. He didn't look up until he'd finished.

'It was like this. With all of them. Arranged. Around them. Like gifts.'

I didn't move any closer. I just looked over at the table.

'Is that what it is Annie?'

I stared. It was like a puzzle and, just like a puzzle, after being foxed by what he'd done I saw it suddenly. Not gifts. It was all arranged, I saw it so plainly.

'Not gifts.' My voice splintered. 'Grave goods.'

Here, at last, was Evan's goodbye message.

Terry Adam looked at me for a long moment. I looked back and he knew his message was delivered. The last of my Evan, speckled and grainy, my memories of the lab, the white and tinny steel of the surfaces. Evan's face intent upon the bones and fragments. His eyes squinting in the sun that day in My Mother's garden, the knots he tied in the twine. The face I had loved and not known.

Evan Bees was going now. We were done. Out at the landfill the bodies were all women, it was written in the set of their pelvises. But now I knew that as they dug they had unearthed what remained of Evan Bees. The careful placing of grave goods. The archaeology of it.

I don't look back. I keep running. Running through the streets and the stitch and spraining my ankle. Run. Run. Past the park. The allotments. Past Dollyville. My breath like knives and all I hear is white noise.

Dig Deep with Arthur:
revelation

Evan Bees sobbed. And I mean sob. Great retching, tearing sobs that were almost silent. Sat on the edge of the bed with his hands palm down, gripping the squared-off edges of the mattress as if he was on the edge of some cliff and would tumble any second. The sobs tore out of him with only eerie gasps and wheezes. As if all the energy was concentrated into his grief, none wasted on wailing or groaning.

Annie Colville talks to the Dead and they come, unbidden, to talk to her. The women, his 'sacrifices', had come back to him through her. One night, about a year after they were married. She was asleep. And they came back to him.

In the morning Annie didn't remember, was tired but didn't remember. She kissed him. But she kissed him now with the mouth of the Dead.

So he vanished. To be away from them, to be where they wouldn't find him. And his punishment is not just the years spent sleeping in doorways and not looking back. His punishment is that he cannot be with Annie.

He sobs. Dribble comes out of his mouth. Snot slithers from his nose. But the only thing he is sorry for is himself.

You don't know about the brain, you know. You don't know about the myriad chemical reactions and the sorcery of emotion. That someone so evil, so culpable, is also capable of love. To me it is the oddities, the failings and the hatefulness that sometimes show us about God. Talk about working in mysterious ways.

So. Annie Bees is her name. Except he kept calling her Annie Colville. He didn't use any of those New Agey terms either for what she does, mediumship or whatever. Nothing spiritual or shamanistic. He put it simply. Concise. Like a job. As if she was customer services or a telephone helpline. She's a blacksmith. A librarian. A baker. No. She talks to the Dead. Or worse, they talk to her without her even asking to be told. They invade her privacy, is how he put it. Annie has no privacy, he said. I think he's wrong. Annie has too much privacy.

Everything she is has been shoved down and muffled. Hiding. Or crowded out with everyone that bustles for her attention.

Either way. Evan Bees couldn't handle Love or Fear or Guilt. So, like any coward, he ran away.

Only washing up here at last, working at uncovering those skeletons, he has learned that you can't hide from what you know. You can hide it from others, but not from yourself. There is no running away.

Fundamental really. Written on the back of a thousand cornflake packets I should think.

Evan Bees is the Undead, too cowardly to die, and yet not quite alive.

It made a circuit for him. The bodies. The grave goods. The uncovering of secrets. Hidden lives. And the lightning was the electricity he generated. God points a finger.

There's a phrase. I think it's French. *Un coup de foudre*. A bolt of lightning. Mostly it's used to talk about love. Love at first sight. The inevitability of a passion. It is probably one of those French sayings that the French never use and most likely didn't invent, like c'est la vie. Whatever. It hit me. Residual charge that day, sitting in that hospital room with the bandaged Evan Bees.

Except it burned me on the inside.

I headed back to the hostel and I packed up my bag. When they'd all trekked out to the pub for the evening I went through Evan's stuff, looking for clues. Looking for the map to Annie. Only the map is not written in his baggage, or in the things he has said. As I am sifting through his humming pants I don't much glance at the newspaper hanging off Andy's bunk. It is only when I stand up too quickly and bang my head on the support that the newspaper flutters to the floor and in picking up the pieces, I read.

Mixed scones

ATALANTA WOKE me. I was under the table in The Glade kitchen. Like a cat. Or Cinderella. She made me some breakfast and as I sat at a table by the window, I watched Brian and the Christmas tree team heading out. Atalanta wanted to bribe me with fresh tea before she started begging me to help out. Aileen was off on her cabinetmaking course and Atalanta wanted some help in the run-up to Christmas.

Goatmill Country Park hosts its own moonlight walk with festive refreshments. There is also a grotto where Santa sees the children. It was very busy now and Atalanta didn't want to have to train up some girl. She wanted a seasoned professional. I thought what she and Brian really wanted was to keep me away from the LookOut and keep me in their sight. Safe in the last lap to December the fifth. I knew I didn't want to go back to the basement. Not ever.

The revelation came in a box of cauliflowers that afternoon.

Police officer killed in knifing tragedy. Constable Terry Adam assisting at a call-out for a domestic dispute saved a young newlywed, Heather Fraser, from the jealous rage of her husband, Richard Fraser. In trying to take a knife off Richard Fraser he was fatally stabbed.

November was ending. December the fifth loomed large on the calendar. I'd had to make an appointment to see the solicitor and we'd talked about the official things that would be done. I did not hope that someone would come forward with a sighting of Evan and delay the process.

I wanted Evan Bees to be legally dead. The fact that he was only legally dead, paper dead, meant he could not come back to tell me what I did not want to hear. If he came back now I could turn him away with a nod, because now I knew. He had not run away because he hated me, because I stifled or suffocated him, because he was a coward or an explorer or wanted to be a woman. He had needed to be gone.

Now, he would be. I wanted Mrs Harper in the post office to check over the details of his passing and, with a huge and efficient hand on her shiny steel stamp, to kerchunk him into the past. Vanish him.

Both Atalanta and Lara offered to accompany me on the day. The night before, as we packed away the last of the mince pies and put the Christmas cakes into tins ready for tomorrow, I said that I wanted to go alone. Lara had the day off, December the fifth was going to be a Wednesday. On the Tuesday night I collected my LookOut leaflets and she let me in at the back door of the library. We stacked them on the table by the door and I told her that it would be fine. It would be an ending to the story as if someone had found the missing page to a whodunnit. Put me out of my misery.

The solicitors' offices were in a huge old mansion once owned by Sir Charles Whitworth's wife's father. Thurston House. The offices don't fit into the grand Georgian rooms. There are partitions and lowered ceilings. Bits of architraving and coving escape in odd corners and the stairs creak. Voices carry, echo and are blanked out suddenly by MDF doors.

I think of all the unfinished business in the corridors here. I think of the divorces and the fights and feuds. I think of all the wills. Messages from the Dead. I want you to do this. I want the Crown Derby to go here. To sit on this sideboard.

No one ever makes a will and says I don't want you to grieve. I want you to wake up tomorrow and be happy. To head out and get on with it. Whatever it is. It's all money and property. No one writes that they loved you. I bequeath you all my love to keep forever. All this, is yours.

I find that my hand is shaking. My hearing seems to be intensified. I can hear a car grinding around as it backs out of the poky carpark at the back of the building. Most disconcerting of all is the chocolate-brown-clad gentleman with mutton-chop whiskers who plummets past the draughty sash window as I hear someone alive laughing at a sudden office joke. A phone is ringing and a muffled voice answers it. The stairs creak.

The solicitor accompanied me downstairs later. She shook my hand and offered some official sympathy. It reminded me of Terry Adam's police smile. Practised. She opened the door. Outside it was raining. I stepped into the rain and started to walk back to The Glade. By the time I got there I was utterly drenched. Atalanta gave me some dry clothes to put on.

I burn the clothes I was wearing. Even the raincoat. Cross over it.

We had a very busy day at The Glade. We sold enough wedges of Victoria sponge to build a dam. Enough scones to cobble the main street. A bath of cream. An ocean of tea. A small boating lake of coffee. That is what I thought about. I thought about the food. About smiling at people and the crispness of the gingham tablecloths. I could smell the fresh flowers in a vase on every table.

That day, I remembered My Mother and I was happy to think about her. On that day it did not make me sad to think about her in her white chef's pinny, her hands floury, her smile never failing no matter how rude the customer. The ruder they were the nicer she was, more smiley, calling them 'love', more small talk. Battering them with her genuine charm. They never won.

There was Mr Hoyle in his greasy homburg hat. Mr Hoyle with his reputation for beating a bear with a sore head in a grumpy competition. Mr Hoyle was a bear with horrendous piles. He rolled into The Glade one afternoon. He had been taking his elderly and equally sour dog, Maxie, for a walk in the woods. He was complaining about the thickness of the milk, the wateriness of the tea, the doughiness of the scones, the stickiness of the jam, the stink of the flowers.

My Mother used a charm offensive to bat back at him. That first day the killer shot was a wink as she brought him a fresh scone, hot from the oven. Why was this woman winking at him? What was going on? Did she have a nervous tic? Was she completely barking mad?

'I don't know, what do you think, Cheeky?' came My Mother's reply before she turned back towards the counter. She enjoyed the reaction. The blustering. But he finished the tea. Scowling. Grumpling.

Next day he was back for more. Back for a fight. How far could he push her before she'd bare her teeth? He was shocking to other people. The bad temper. The ill manners. The girls all got used to it in time, although once or twice there were tears.

My Mother told them straight: you cry in the kitchen. Don't give him the satisfaction. She'd leave them mopping their tears with a teatowel as she faced him off.

'Anything to follow, Mr Hoyle? We've got some of that farmhouse fruit cake you hated three times last week,' she'd offer with a smile. The tea was never right. 'Tastes like cat's piss,' he'd say.

'You a connoisseur? Drink a lot of cat's piss do you Mr Hoyle?' replied My Mother.

'I do here,' he'd grumble.

The hot water wasn't hot enough. The milk not milky enough. My Mother had a reply for everything. Snap and crackle. He never won. She was never rude to him. And he tried very hard.

When she died Mr Hoyle sat at his usual table for eight hours straight and didn't say a single word other than to bark his order at the waitress. Zoë. Who had corkscrew-curled red hair. He opened the paper but didn't read it. At the end of the day he put his cash on the counter and walked out.

Mr Hoyle is still alive. He is in his eighties now and his daughter has tried to stop him coming. He isn't supposed to eat cream teas. As he has said, the thought of his cream tea twice a week is all that keeps him alive. He walks up here from town.

After closing we ate together. Atalanta and the other girl, Min, and myself. It wasn't a celebration or a wake. It was tea. Then Atalanta ran me to the LookOut in her car. We were clearing out my things. The sweater on the back of the chair was mouldy with damp and full of chewed holes. Everything I possessed didn't fill the empty shoebox. I had lived there like a rat.

Just as I was leaving, Florrie came through the wall. She took her coat and this time we headed out together. Only I wouldn't be back.

*

I lie down in the old lodge that Brian used to share with My Mother, and Evan Bees is blurred in a dream. The woman is my nightmare. She wakes me up. It seems very dark here. The bulb has gone on the bedside lamp while I have been asleep. I am afraid. Afraid of the sudden dark. Afraid of where I might be. Maybe at last I'm in that Waiting Room.

No. She was shaking me, shaking me awake.

'Listen. The middle one. The middle one was his. Tell him. Tell him.' And as I finally found my torch and flicked the switch I only had a moment to see her face before she was gone. I didn't know her. And let's face it, how was I ever going to know who 'him' was? I called out but it was useless. And I found myself laughing at the prospect of Him Night.

In the morning I woke up at six. The old lady was so quiet sitting there that I didn't see her until I was moving out towards the bathroom. I stood in the doorway, turned. She smiled at me. I noticed she was knitting.

'The trouble with being dead…your knitting never grows.'

I had never seen her before although her voice seemed famil-iar. I hear so many voices. Ha. And I still think I'm sane. She smoothed the knitting and put it in a bag made from old curtain materials with clacky wooden handles.

'I've a message for you…' Uh-oh, another Him, I thought. 'Does it involve…'

'Crown Derby tableware? No. It's about Arthur.'

I had a vague memory of an evening at Hackett Lane Spirit-ualist Church when someone I couldn't see kept saying the name. When for once we were all searching for an Arthur instead of a Jim.

'You'll know him when you see him. He has one eye. Wears a patch. When he gets here you go up to him and you say, "I'm her, I'm the one." That's all. Tell him Gran sent you. He'll know.'

'Where will I see him? Do you know where I can find him? Or would you like me to place a small ad?'

'No. You'll tell him to his face. He'll come. It's been a long time coming love, but he's on his way now. Then you tell him. I know I can rely on you.'

She smiled, picked up the knitting and turned to go.

'You didn't wake me.'

She looked up at me, raised her eyebrows, questioning.

'Why didn't you wake me?' I asked her outright.

'You were sleeping, love.'

She said it as if it was the simplest thing in the universe. Then she was gone. I headed to work. I did not want to keep them waiting.

We had a Christmas lunch booked in, not your usual turkey. This was a simpler affair with sandwiches and quiches, mince pies and Christmas cake. It was the old folks' club from the park. They arrived in two coaches, swathed in scarves and wearing galoshes. Galoshes that could probably be classified as antiques, all sorts of boots and footwear that in some cases had lasted through a world war and the Suez Crisis. Handbags from the days when crocodiles were a fashion accessory.

They didn't adulterate the tea and coffee with alcohol, they just asked for clean glasses. There was music from four chaps who had been quite a famous folk group. The Turnip Townshends. It was busy. There was laughter. The kitchen was hot and damp and filled with vanilla and brandy aromas. Atalanta asked me to open the window and the frosted December day cut in. Outside it was sunny, that cold golden sun. Outside Goatmill Country Park smelt of leaf mould and open air.

Arthur was outside. Just standing there waiting as I came out with the bin bags. Lifting them up high, because the bins were too tall for me really. I'd kept telling Atalanta that we needed a step up. I felt my muscles working. Satisfying. Fleshy. One of those odd moments when you feel that however idiotic it seems, this is a life skill. The knack of swinging the big black bin bag into the tall black bin. Flicking the lid back over and just catching it with your free hand so that it doesn't bang shut. The engineering of it. The physics.

Clearly I needed a hobby.

He'd been watching me. Just standing there watching. I startled a little as he appeared in the periphery of my vision. I stopped. Thinking for just a moment that I looked scruffy. Smelled, in fact. He was looking away to one side, uncertain he'd come to the right place. I thought he was after the job. Brian had advertised. So here he was, at the wrong lodge.

'You after the job?'

It was then that he turned full face and I saw the eye patch. After that. Well. Adrenalin glands emptying. Fuelling my memory so that as long as I live I will never forget the moment Arthur looked round at me with his one eye. Green. Chocolate brown. Gold. I didn't get to see the gold until much later. To see the gold you have to be up close.

Which is a motto really isn't it?

His clothes. Green. Earth brown. All the colours of the forest so that if you turned your head he could disappear back into the trees, into the landscape. Belong. Have I ever looked like that? I've spent my whole life feeling like the sore thumb. His boots, muddy and well used but well cared for.

'Yes. I'm after the job,' he replied. Soft voice. Eye very direct, looking right at you and searching. Having a bloody good look at me. That is how he is, though. Arthur can tell more about you from the curve of your eyebrow, the lick of your lips.

What is the difference between warning and advice? She had told me he would come and now here he was. This was new.

This was more scary. A message for me. Hard to imagine anything more scary than my life had been already. Arthur and his one eye. I had the message from Gran but I couldn't blurt it out then. He didn't look like he would believe me. He didn't look the type. He wasn't needy or asking. He just turned up.

She woke me up that night. Cross.

'He's here and you didn't tell him. Get on with it. You need to do this.'

I was awake now. No going back to sleep.

'How many years have you been doing this, lovey? I thought you were an old hand.'

'Too many years. Very old hand. That's why I didn't tell him.'

'Get on with it. Never mind editing the highlights.'

As she turned to go there was a gentleman standing there in a chocolate brown frock coat. She took him by the elbow as she moved away. Bustled him along with her. 'You can forget it, lovey. She needs her kip.'

The room was quiet after that. And I did go back to sleep.

Arthur. We existed for a while in the closed world of the park. Arthur learned fast. Every evening Brian came in with some tale about what they've been doing, how Arthur is up on every bird and beetle. Arthur doesn't see a bird. He sees a wren. A greenfinch. Arthur looks in a hedgerow and sees the wild-life. This is all Brian requires of anyone. That they don't see the wood, or even the trees. That they see the oak gall and the hawkmoth.

I just listened in as Brian talked with Atalanta. Brian knew he had found his heir to the kingdom, the land of the Giant. That's how I came to know Arthur at first. I picked up the fairy stories.

After that, it was as simple as being in the same room together. He didn't say, I didn't say, and that said everything. We had never met and yet there was some spark of recognition when our eyes met. One day, I found some courage, rolled into a linty ball in my apron pocket.

'What colour was your other eye?' I asked, for a dare, as I brought his extra-hot water and the milk jug.

'Sky blue pink with a yellow border,' he growled deadpan and I dropped the milk jug because that's something My Mother used to say.

I realised very slowly that he's the man with the spotted handkerchief and the bit of cheese. The woodcutter who comes at last to save Red Riding Hood.

He had a habit of sitting quietly at the back with a plate of mixed scones and a pot of tea. There was no one else in that day. It had been raining hard through the night and just kept going. Arthur's hair was slicked back off his face and he gave off a niff of damp dog. I liked to be near him so to keep him there I brought, unbidden, a pot of hot water to freshen the tea. That's when I saw her. His gran. She wasn't knitting this time, unless you count her brow. Her lips were pursed and prune-like, disapproving.

'If you want it doing, do it your bloody self,' is all she said to me before she leeched into me and I was pins and needles all over. Arthur was in the middle of splitting a sultana scone and putting jam on it as her voice came out of me.

'Arthur. Listen to me, this is her, she's the one, make no bones about it. Stop fannying about the pair of you.' And she was gone. I tumbled like a felled tree, knocking the table behind me over. Unconscious, wearing a jammed scone like a dainty hat.

He was so still that the jam slid off the knife onto his hand. Onto that fleshy bit at the bottom of his thumb. Looked like blood. He didn't wipe it off as he knelt beside me, picked me up. We were jam everywhere, making us stick together. Hello, message anyone? Yoo-hoo.

He revived me with tea. Sat me in one of the bentwood chairs while he finished the washing up. Then he stood beside me. I looked into his face, the few greys in the slick of his hair, the one eye, the slightly grubby look of his skin and I knew. His one eye just looked at me. Reeled me in. Hypnotic. Cycloptic.

'Ready?' he said.

I was ready for anything.

He was living in one of the bird hides at the edge of the lake. Brian suspected, but a man who has spent a few years of his life being the Man Fox has a deeper understanding. We walked through the late afternoon, on into the wood. I wondered which of us would speak first. In the end he just held out his hand. Doesn't get much simpler than that. Not that I took his hand. I looked at it. Walked past it along the path towards the bird hide. As if it was just a sign post. This Way.

At the bird hide we didn't talk. We watched a heron at the lakeside. Watched him for what seemed like seconds but must have been hours. It grew dark. Dark so that we couldn't see the heron anymore. Couldn't see each other.

In the dark he leaned to me, his lips moving against my cheek as he whispered, 'This is her. She's the One.'

It was cool and damp in the morning at the bird hide. We had breakfast at The Glade. Arthur helping me with a batch of early-morning scones. A skill acquired from Gran. We ate them hotly buttered. Not saying anything much. I didn't know what I felt. Slightly crumpled from our night of love in the bird hide. Earthen.

Then it struck me, as wild and painful and illuminating as lightning. We were in the middle of an understanding silence.

Which is when I started to cry, tears hotter than the scone, more meltingly salty than the butter.

He didn't look away. He smoothed at them with his thumb. Licked the thumb. I sobbed my heart into his green jacket. Not once did he utter a cliché or a hackneyed 'it's all right'. Not even a 'there, there'. Just the tight, safe, circle of his arms and the steady rhythm of his breathing.

My premium bonds. Bought with the money from Aunt Mag's Thursdays. One came up. A million pounds prize money looked mythical and small, the solitary '1' and the empty row of '0's when I got the cheque. A flimsy bit of paper. Until I bought Goatmill Park with Brian and his life savings. No dolly houses here. Instead we're building Scandinavian lodges. Just a few, for those, like me, who like to live in their shed. We have the keys to our kingdom. We can lock the gates.

Arthur is building our lodge. He thinks there's a defensive magic in doing that, in putting his sweat, his hairs, his skin into the log walls. I think of Mrs Berry.

He isn't scared of me. Not even after his gran and our first night in the bird hide when they woke me, the first, male voice, urgent, whispering over and over. Pitch bloody black in that bird hide.

'Annie,' he said, 'Annie,' and I couldn't answer. I was piled under them. He reached for me. Even with one eye he could see I was the one speaking, that the voices were coming out of me.

It was a bad night. They come in the daytime, bad time, all the time but that first night my defences were down. As soon as I let that happen they bustle in like it's the January sale.

They washed in and over, wave on wave of voices. Like a radio tuning in. Like white noise. I could see him but I couldn't reach out. I waited for him to turn tail, to scream or run or drop dead, but he didn't do any of that. He moved over so we were spooned together, his big callused hand on my hip as they raged and poured into the dark.

I fit so neatly into the arch of his body, it's like he is my carapace. He listens for a moment, to what they have to say and then he whispers, like a low breeze into my ear. 'On your way. You're not going anywhere sunshine and she needs her kip.'

Someone at the back, the plummeting man with the mutton-chop whiskers says, 'What?' but they fall almost silent, talking amongst themselves. 'What did he say?' 'How rude.' 'Sssshhhhh.'

Arthur. He wrestles their door shut for now, and I sleep.